GHOSTLY WITNESSES

HIDDEN SECRETS FROM THE PAST

JAMES L WILLIAMS

The Book Guild Ltd

First published in Great Britain in 2017 by
The Book Guild Ltd
9 Priory Business Park
Wistow Road, Kibworth
Leicestershire, LE8 0RX
Freephone: 0800 999 2982
www.bookguild.co.uk
Email: info@bookguild.co.uk
Twitter: @bookguild

Copyright © 2017 James L Williams

The right of James L Williams to be identified as the author of this
work has been asserted by him in accordance with the
Copyright, Design and Patents Act 1988.

All rights reserved. No part of this publication may be
reproduced, transmitted, or stored in a retrieval system, in any form or by any means,
without permission in writing from the publisher, nor be otherwise circulated in
any form of binding or cover other than that in which it is published and without
a similar condition being imposed on the subsequent purchaser.

This work is entirely fictitious and bears no resemblance to any persons living or dead.

Cover illustration by Mike Bastin, at MikeBastinCreative.com

Typeset in Minion Pro

Printed and bound in Great Britain by CPI Group (UK) Ltd, Croydon, CR0 4YY

ISBN 978 1912083 657

British Library Cataloguing in Publication Data.
A catalogue record for this book is available from the British Library.

*Ron Hewlett and his wife Win, for encouraging me to move to Bristol in the early 70's and for giving me quality support and advice when things became difficult.
Better friends would be harder to find.
R.I.P Ron, you always said it like it was with no holds barred.*

ACKNOWLEDGEMENT

Helen Sage and June Totterdell for their help in completing the final editing process.

1

Bloody kids! Where were they hiding in this rabbit warren of streets? They probably know the area better than me anyway.

Even though Constable Vic Holland had moved to the town of Clapfield some six months earlier he found himself drawn into unfamiliar territory. With other disadvantages apart from his lack of precise local knowledge he was loathe to admit any of these facts. He had allowed himself to become overweight and out of condition since being transferred from his last post.

He had been on the verge of being promoted to sergeant before his transfer but a series of unfortunate incidents in his personal life had curtailed his rise through the ranks.

Pausing to catch his breath and listen for any noises, all he could hear was his own panting and the chiming of a distant church clock. Just to add to his discomfort, the swirling mist from the river was getting denser by the minute and the inadequate street lighting only seemed to heighten, not lessen the gloom.

Which way had those sods gone, he asked himself. The officer had been on his way home and was about to call in the chip shop for his supper when the two thugs ran out of a nearby shop they had broken into and started a fire inside, knocking down a pregnant woman and her husband in their escape. Pausing only briefly to check the two victims were not seriously hurt, he gave chase. Within a very short period Vic discovered he had strayed into an area of the town he had never ventured into previously.

No more just telling kids off for not having lights on their bikes or investigating which farmer had let his sheep escape to graze and leave their droppings on the local golf course. Or so he had envisaged on leaving his last post in the rural West Midlands. Ever since arriving in Clapfield his daily routine seemed to have consisted of tracing the owners of lost pets and mundane traffic duties and school patrols. Vic was convinced the duty sergeant had taken an instant dislike to him.

"This division of the Clapfield force needs alert and fit officers to keep ahead of the local tearaways, not overweight country bumpkins," had been Sergeant Proudfoot's greeting when they had first met, "and until you get some of that podge off you, Holland, I won't embarrass the local community more than the absolute minimum with your presence."

The only change from this routine had occurred within two weeks of arriving in his new surroundings. A body had been spotted on the banks of the local river and Vic, the only available officer at the time, had been dispatched to help the Fire and Rescue services to retrieve the man's corpse.

It was evident from its condition that the body had been in the river for a long time; the stench of the rotting corpse was too much for Vic's stomach and he threw up on the river bank. This event was relayed back to his station and he had to face several days of ribbing from his colleagues.

A post mortem was held which Vic had to attend. The man had been missing for over a year and was known to take late night walks along the river bank after visiting local pubs.

The jury in the post mortem hearing reached the conclusion that the man, Graham Bishop, had drunk too much one night and fallen into the river. The coroner's verdict was accidental death.

Even after only such a short period in his new surroundings Vic had felt like asking for a transfer back to his old patch. But he knew he couldn't return there, everyone was talking about his disastrous marriage. Fiona, his now deceased wife, had not only embarked on an illicit affair with one of her clients, she had come to an untimely end with her lover in bizarre circumstances. The story of their demise had made national press headlines.

If he could catch these two thugs even colleagues like Sgt Proudfoot might see him in a different light. There had been numerous break-ins and incidents of intimidation amongst the business section of the town going back for several years. Suspects had been questioned, mainly from the local Youth Centre, but on each occasion alibis were always found and no further action taken.

A faint scratching sound reached his ears and he held his breath for a moment, trying to locate its source. An alleyway loomed ahead on his left and he took a couple of steps towards it. He peered into the gloom and listened for the sound he had heard moments earlier. It resumed a few seconds later. Vic advanced into the darkness and was greeted by the clatter of a dustbin lid falling to the ground followed seconds later by a startled cat darting past him into the night.

Vic cursed under his breath. That cat might have nine lives but he didn't and moments like that weren't welcome.

"Hey, you fat pig, you looking for us?"

Turning to see where the call had come from, it took Vic a couple of seconds to spot the figure in the shop doorway some twenty yards away.

For a moment, he forgot his basic training instincts about being lured into unfamiliar surroundings unless someone was in immediate danger, or if he was outnumbered in any way.

The youth disappeared into the darkened building and Vic

followed seconds later. In his keenness to apprehend the youths, he failed to notice that the windows were boarded up and had several old posters partly covering or hanging from the wood panels.

Stopping just inside the doorway to accustom his eyes to the darkness, Vic became aware of two things that should have warned him of impending danger. It seemed even colder inside the building, with a down draft of air adding to the chill. There was also a smell of burning wood. No, not burning but burnt wood. A fire had taken place here sometime in the past. That could mean an unsafe floor at the very least.

There was a street light near the corner of the next road which was flickering vigorously and then went out completely. Cursing himself for not having a torch in his possession Vic moved cautiously towards the centre of the room and listened for any sound that might pinpoint the two villains.

A soft whistle to his right caught his attention and he turned to check its source. A blinding beam of light shone into his eyes and he raised a hand to deflect the glare. At the same time his feet moved involuntarily backwards onto some unsafe floorboards. They might have withstood someone of a lesser weight or stature than Vic but the sudden pressure, added to their long period of neglect, proved too much for the joist and boards.

A single snapping sound was the only warning noise; even so, it came too late to save the policeman from disappearing up to his waist into the floor space. Even though he had only fallen about three feet into the void, the shock was enough to wind him momentarily.

The boards had snapped into many pieces and the splinters of wood that remained on the edges of the unbroken boards caught on his uniform. Sensing that he was in danger if he remained where he was he struggled to extract himself. However, before he had time to escape from the hole, Vic was set upon by his tormentors.

With cries of delight and triumph they began aiming kicks at his upper body and head. The blows came so quickly he could only just fend off those aimed at his face and head. Fortunately for Vic, the youths were only wearing soft trainer shoes, otherwise they could have inflicted even more damage.

One attacker got a little too confident in their victim's lack of mobility and tried feigning a blow to Vic's head, with the intention of aiming another kick with his other foot.

More by luck than anything else, Vic managed to catch hold of the foot of his attacker and with both hands twisted the foot, causing the youth to fall over onto his back. Vic felt a badge of some kind on the heel of the footwear as he tried to remove the shoe, with the hope of making at least one of the assailants less mobile, but the youth, while shouting a torrent of obscenities, managed to scramble out of his reach.

The second attacker, not realising his friend was on the floor, had stopped to catch his breath. This brief respite allowed Vic time to try and extract himself from his temporary prison. He tried to push up with both hands but his left foot was stuck firmly in the muddy earth below the flooring. Before he could make another attempt to raise himself the light was shone in his eyes and Vic was forced to raise a hand to deflect the glare. Moments later a sharp blow from a large piece of wood dealt Vic a glancing blow across the back of his unprotected upper shoulders and neck. Shouts of anger and pain from their victim only helped the assailants into finding their target in the darkness.

Both were now armed with pieces of wood and landed blow after blow on the policeman's arms, shoulders and back. He kept his head and face protected by leaning forwards. However, he knew he couldn't remain in such a vulnerable position for much longer without sustaining serious injury. If he couldn't lift himself out of the hole, then maybe it would be possible to find temporary protection below the floorboards. There was about four inches of clinging mud in which his boots were stuck but he calculated there must be more than two feet of space between the mud and the floor joists.

As the blows continued to rain down on his back Vic tried to move his feet in an effort to release them from the clinging morass. After what seemed an age, first one, and then the other foot squelched free. The blows had suddenly become less frequent as one of the assailants paused to catch his breath but his companion moved around so as to vary the direction of attack and try to deliver a blow to Vic from an unexpected direction.

"C'mon, Torch, it was your idea to get him in here, so do your bloody share!" yelled the youth who had continued the attack; now he too paused for a moment's relief.

Seizing his opportunity, Vic started to lower himself further into the hole. He would have succeeded before the youths could grasp what his intentions were had his coat not become snagged on a splintered piece of floorboard. Vic wasted vital seconds trying to release himself, finally resorting to pulling away the snagged material with a ripping sound that seemed to echo around the building. A brief flash of the torch light alerted the youths to the source. In an instant the assault was resumed with even more vigour than before.

With only one arm free to protect his face, a couple of blows from the wooden weapons caught Vic more strikes to his upper back and shoulders before he was able to disappear below floor level. He scrambled blindly away from the hole to avoid any possibility of the youths reaching him. The thick mud and his own bulk made progress in the confined space even more difficult. His hopes for an escape route ended abruptly when he banged his head against the retaining wall and he let out a short curse.

Seconds later the torch beam was shone into the hole.

"Can you see him, Torch?" a squeaky voice asked.

"He's not near the hole anyway, and I ain't about to stick my head down there in case he belts me one. Find me something to burn, Keys. I'll show you how to turn that fat pig into smoky bacon," replied the second youth with an unmistakable Yorkshire accent.

"Let's leave him, Torch. Beating up a copper is bad enough but murder isn't in my game plan," said the one called Keys.

"If he gets out of here we'll both go down for a long stretch. No one will find him in here for months by which time you and me will be long gone. Stop wasting time and find me something to burn. Take the torch and check out the back room, there's a pile of junk in one corner, some of that should do the trick."

All of this conversation reached Vic's ears and a feeling of panic began to grip him. He managed to turn around in his confined space to face the hole he had come through. He tried to keep the fear out of his voice as he called out,

"OK you two, you've had your fun. Like your mate said, knocking me about is one thing, but attempted murder of a police officer will bring the whole of the Clapfield force on your case. They'll catch you sooner or later, and remember, cop killers don't have such an easy time in prison."

"You still awake down there in your mud bath, you fat pig? You're not the first I've smoked you know, no one's caught me yet and they never will. Hurry up Keys you bloody cripple, we haven't got all night!"

"Lay off, Torch, It's your fault I've only one good hand. This stuff will have to do, I want to get out of here, this place gives me the creeps," moaned Keys as he returned.

"What's up, scared of ghosts?" laughed Torch.

Vic moved as quietly as he could to the hole in the floor. He would have to act quickly to have any chance of escaping. Fortunately the two youths were too busy preparing their kindling to notice his movements in the darkness. The smell below ground was also starting to have an effect on Vic as well as the discomfort from his wounds.

Torch gathered together the small pile of rubbish that his friend had brought him, next to the hole in the floor. He took an aerosol can from one of his pockets and a lighter from another. He sprayed some of the contents of the can over the rubbish and then told his friend to stand back.

"When this catches light, use that piece of wood and push it into the hole. Enjoy your last smoke, copper," he called out to Vic.

He took one pace back and aimed the aerosol at the rubbish once more. Holding the lighter just in front of the can, he was careful not to splash himself with its contents and lit his lighter. Acting like a mini flame-thrower it engulfed the rubbish in a mass of fire. With the use of the wooden clubs the second youth pushed the small bonfire into the hole.

At the same moment, there was a loud clattering sound near one corner of the room, followed by another as a couple of bricks fell from above. With a startled yelp Keys dropped his club and ran for the door.

"Come on Torch, the bloody place is caving in, leave the copper or we'll be joining him if this place comes down."

Hesitating only momentarily, his friend followed him out. In his haste Torch failed to realise that the lighter had fallen from his pocket.

As soon as the flaming mass landed in the mud next to Vic it began to smoke, but the flames continued to burn. Frantically scooping the wet mud onto the flames he started to choke in the confined space as it quickly filled with smoke. The flames soon died down but such was their bulk, Vic would have to push the rubbish out of the way if he was to escape. It would have been safer to push the mass away with his feet using the protection of his regulation footwear. However, there was no time to manoeuvre himself around in the confined space to do this. Every second was vital if he wasn't to succumb to the smoke.

Even though most of the smoke was escaping through the hole in the floor, Vic's eyes were watering and his coughing increased as he fought for breath. Scooping two large handfuls of mud, he used them as a protective barrier for his hands as he desperately pushed the mound of smouldering rubbish away from his escape route. It took three attempts to clear enough space for him to reach fresher air and sanctuary. Precious but necessary seconds were taken up by covering his hands with fresh mud to protect them from the worst of the heat. Even with this covering he could feel his hands begin to blister but the pain only spurred him on to even greater efforts to escape from this death trap.

At last he could feel the cold air above his head, which indicated the way out was directly above him. He knew he only had the strength to make one attempt to get out. His breaths were coming in short gasps and the pain from the combination of the blisters and the beating he had taken earlier were fuzzing his thoughts. In his keenness to reach fresh air Vic half jumped, half dived for the opening. He had only exited as far as his upper chest when he was pulled back violently to end up on his knees in the mud and hot ash, with only his head and outstretched arms out of the hole. Once again, his coat had caught on one of the broken floorboards and impeded his progress.

Vic didn't want to fight any more. With his face on the floor and one arm in front of him and the other by his side in the hole he just wanted to rest for a while. Sod the smoke, those kids, the Force, his ex-wife, he just needed some rest.

He was only vaguely aware of two strong bony hands reaching under his armpits and lifting him effortlessly out of the hole. He was placed in a sitting position against the wall near the doorway and seconds later felt something cold being put on his hands.

"You're safe now. Your friends will be here soon," said a tall thin man in a deep but gentle voice. Vic tried to look at his saviour but all he saw was a figure disappear into the gloom.

Before passing out he vaguely heard the sound of approaching sirens.

2

"You've had a lucky escape, Holland. Another couple of minutes in that smoke and you'd have been a goner," declared Inspector Stevens as he stood next to the hospital bed. He continued, "the doctors have said you should be OK after a few days rest, and only try to talk as little as possible. But I need to know who were the scum responsible for this. Can you remember anything that will help?"

"Just two kids wearing the usual gear, Sir; jeans, trainers, bomber jackets, that kind of thing," Vic croaked, and started coughing again for the umpteenth time.

The inspector waited patiently until the coughing had subsided and then remarked, "That's about as much as the man and woman who were knocked over outside the shop those two broke into could remember. Pity no one else saw them; as usual, when we need the public's help they're not around to give it."

"Didn't the shop owner manage to get a look at them? I could have sworn there was someone else in the shop apart from those two thugs."

"No, because nothing of value was stolen he didn't want to make a statement. He's not the first person to decline to help, possibly scared of any repercussions," Stevens said in a resigned tone.

"What about the old man who helped me get out of the hole, Sir? If it hadn't been for him, I'd still be stuck in that place," Vic said, and took another couple of sips of water to ease his aching throat.

"According to the fire brigade, the only person in the area was the woman from across the road who saw smoke coming from the building and two figures running away. But no male of any description. Whoever he was, I'd like to have a chat with him as well. I'll get the investigating officer to make enquiries. Anyway, Holland, I have to go now. Glad to see things weren't more serious. Look forward to having you back on duty once you've recovered," said the inspector as he turned to leave.

"Thanks for coming in, Sir," replied Vic and sat back wondering who his mystery saviour was, and why he hadn't stayed or at least left his name to be contacted later. His thoughts were disturbed by the arrival of a doctor.

"Good morning, Mr Holland, how are you feeling now?"

"A bit sore on my back and shoulders, a sore head and this irritating cough that won't go away," Vic replied. "Oh, and my hands are tingling a bit," he added and started coughing once more.

"Hopefully that cough will go in a few days, but just to be on the safe side, I'll give you some tablets to fight off any possible infection. Can I have a look at your hands please?"

The doctor cut away the dressing on Vic's hands and let out a little gasp of surprise at what he saw. "Either you're a super fast healing person, or there were some magic properties in that cream that was on your hands when you came in last night. Who put the cream on and how did you get those burns?" asked the doctor.

Vic explained how he received his injuries and continued, "I can only guess that it must have been the paramedics or fire brigade who put the cream on. Unless it was the old man."

The doctor shook his head. "I was on duty when you came into Casualty last night and according to the ambulance crew the cream was already on your hands when they got there. The fire brigade didn't put it on, they, as far as I know don't use such stuff. In fact, I've never seen that cream before and I've dealt with several burn cases in my time here. Who was this old man you mentioned?"

It was Vic's turn to look confused and he didn't reply to the doctor's query. Noting his patient's puzzlement the doctor continued, "Never mind for now, Mr Holland. What I can't understand is this. Even though you said you used wet mud to protect your hands against the heat, there was no trace of mud on your hands last night, only that cream. What's more, the cuffs on your coat were burnt away and with that amount of heat I would have expected to have been dealing with second degree burns at the very least. Whatever that cream was, I'd love to get my hands on lots more. I've never seen anything work so fast in my twelve years in medical practice. Anyway, there's no need to put another dressing on, the fresh air will help it heal just as quickly."

He stopped to write some notes in a file and continued to give Vic a full examination before declaring, "I'll send you down for some X-rays this afternoon just to make sure nothing is broken. Although let's say, your puppy fat might have saved you from more serious damage but I want to be sure. You've got a couple of stitches in those gashes on your head and the headaches should go in time. I'll send a nurse with some pain killers. Just rest for now, Mr Holland. Good morning."

"When can I go home, Doctor?" asked Vic.

"Let's see the results of the X-rays first then we'll discuss it." And he left his patient to ponder over the events of the previous night.

Vic took a careful look at his hands and was amazed to see not even one blister on them. Looking at his hands reminded him of the drama and especially the heat he had felt through the coat of mud and he again tried to form an image of the man who, he was convinced, had saved him. Or did he only imagine that part of the drama. A person's mind can sometimes play tricks on them at such times.

But why could he remember nearly every detail up to the point where he was kneeling inside the hole with no apparent strength left to climb out. Then nothing between that point and someone telling him his friends were coming. He was one hundred per cent sure it hadn't been one of the rescue services speaking to him. However, the harder he tried to think the more his head pounded. Vic was grateful when the nurse brought him the painkillers and announced that lunch would be served in about half an hour. He suddenly felt hungry, as his last meal had been over eighteen hours ago. Yet when the meal was put in front of him Vic's appetite had disappeared and after pushing the food around his plate for a couple of minutes he called the orderly to take it away. He could only put this down to all the smoke he had inhaled and dozed off until he was woken up to go for his X-rays.

The results showed there were no broken bones, just severe bruising, mostly on his upper back and shoulders. Despite these optimistic signs the doctor advised Vic to stay in for one more night until his bouts of coughing had subsided. Since he would be going home to an empty flat Vic eventually agreed.

After a light salad, which he reluctantly admitted to himself was his first in years and quite appetizing, two of his work colleagues called in for a brief visit. There was the inevitable leg-pulling and merciless comment about Vic's weight being the only reason for the floor giving way under him. Unfortunately they couldn't report any progress on the investigation into who the attackers might be.

One other surprise awaited him before he dropped off to sleep. His late night drink of tea with milk and two sugars, as he had been used to for countless years, was far too sweet for him and he drank only a couple of mouthfuls before putting it to one side. Almost inevitably the events of the previous night came back in his dreams. Yet with one subtle difference.

> He was back in the building but was looking down on events as they unfolded, but only from the moments prior to his rescue. Firstly, he could see himself crouched in the hole with the smoke billowing around. There was no mud on his hands, just burnt flesh. Something shining on the floor caught his attention but he couldn't focus on it properly.
> Now he was sitting up against the wall with someone crouching over him. This person spoke only once. "You're safe now. Your friends are on their way."
> The figure stood up and walked out of the room. He was tall with grey hair and wore horn-rimmed glasses; Vic thought he looked about seventy.
> Suddenly the scene changed. Vic was in a well-lit room with countless jars and bottles on shelves. His attention was drawn to three photographs on one wall. The first was of a man, probably in his mid-fifties with a little girl on his lap. The second photo was of a girl in her teens on a ski slope, with the same striking red hair as the little girl in the first picture. The third photograph was of a very attractive young woman dressed in her academic robes with what Vic presumed to be a diploma of some kind. Suddenly he felt an arm on his shoulder and a nurse asked him if he wanted his early morning cup of tea.

This time he took only one sugar, still finding it too sweet but he managed to finish it. Breakfast consisted of cereals and toast which to his surprise, filled him up. Not to worry he thought, tomorrow I can have my usual fry-up.

The doctor came to see him soon after breakfast and pronounced Vic fit enough to go home but to rest for a couple of days before visiting his own GP to get the all clear. Since today was Friday Vic would have been due to start a series on night shifts for the next four nights, which he didn't mind missing. Fortunately, one of his colleagues had called at his flat and collected some spare clothes since most of those he had been wearing during that dramatic night were only fit for the rag bag. The doctor had given him a couple of tablets in case of infection from the smoke inhalation and a prescription to get more from a local chemist. Vic summoned a taxi and dropped the prescription at a chemist's on the way home. The pharmacist apologised for not having the tablets in stock but assured Vic a fresh supply would arrive later that day and he would personally deliver them to his flat after closing the shop.

3

The only mail awaiting him in the locked mailbox in the foyer were a monthly motoring magazine and two bills which he collected and then wearily climbed the two flights of stairs to his flat.

Having been brought up to be reliant on nobody except himself, Vic's flat resembled nothing like the average bachelor's apartment. Everything was neatly in its correct place, no magazines scattered around, the bed freshly made, no washing-up waiting to be done and the food cupboards well stocked.

That wasn't the case when he was married to Fiona. She had been too busy cheating on him to care about such mundane things. After he had complained for the fourth time about the lack of cleanliness in their house things suddenly began to improve. It was only when he called briefly at the house that Vic discovered a stranger doing the ironing. Fiona had hired this woman to do all the cleaning and other chores while she carried on her deceptions. Until then his suspicions had never been aroused.

When he was first transferred to Clapfield, Vic had been placed in temporary accommodation which did little to raise his spirits. Limited cooking space, no laundry facilities, which would mean a twice weekly visit to the local launderette, and a pokey bathroom that was too cramped to suit his needs.

Fortunately, on his first walking tour around the area he came across an advert for a two bedroom flat that seemed to offer far more in the way of home comforts. He visited the letting agency at the first opportunity and arranged a viewing of the property which proved to have both positive and negative aspects to its availability.

On the good side, the flat was ideal in its locality to work and had all the facilities and nearby amenities he desired. The flat was only partially furnished so there would be the opportunity to have his own belongings brought out of storage.

On the negative side he was told there were several other people who were showing interest in acquiring the property and the owner, who was out of the country at present, would have the final decision on who was going to be the next tenant; in addition, each applicant would need to fill in a personal questionnaire for the appraisal of the landlord. Vic was not sure if he wanted to wait or to give too much detail of his past to a total stranger.

But he had a good feeling about the apartment, even going in through the downstairs entrance door to the converted house gave him a sensation of entering a welcoming, homely atmosphere and because of this feeling he decided to express his interest in the flat but had set a time limit of four weeks to hear if any progress had been made in his interest.

Much to his surprise and delight he was informed by the letting agency within two weeks that he had been successful in his application. With the help of colleagues both from his previous and current work locations he was able to move in by the end of the month. However, since taking up residence he had never met or even heard anyone in the flat on the ground floor.

Within a month of moving into the apartment Vic received

news that the house he shared with Fiona had been sold and he would be notified of the final amount which would be paid in due course. When the money finally arrived he treated himself to a new car and banked the rest.

He had toyed with the thought of enquiring with the letting agency if the landlord would sell him the apartment but he never seemed to have time to follow up his idea. He had decided to wait and see if he passed his annual medical which he knew was due in a few months and then make a decision on the apartment.

Finding the flat a little on the cold side he switched on the central heating to take off the chill and after making a cup of coffee settled down to watch some television for a while. On every other occasion the flat would have warmed up nicely within about fifteen minutes. But not today. It didn't take him long to notice that the area around his favourite armchair seemed colder than anywhere else in the room and wasn't getting any warmer.

He moved to the two-seater settee which was partly draped in sunlight. This was more like it he thought. Not for long. It took about two minutes for this area to cool down to the same chilly feeling that had surrounded his last resting place. Once more he occupied the armchair after satisfying himself that the temperature on the room thermostat was still set at 20 degrees centigrade.

Once again that part of the room cooled and he had to move back to the settee. This went on for over an hour before Vic admitted defeat and put on another jumper and finally managed to find a comfortable seating position.

He wasn't sure how long he had dozed off for but the street lights shone through the window and on the wet road below, as he awoke to a persistent ringing sound. It took a few seconds for him to identify the sound as that of his bell on the door intercom. Probably one of the lads from the station coming to see if I'm OK, he assumed, and thought about going out for a drink.

The lady smiled as she handed over the packet to Vic. "I'm sorry for the delay, Mr Holland. There was a last minute rush at the shop. If you need any more you'll have to ask your GP for a repeat prescription. The dosage instructions are on the bottle. Thank you, goodnight," she chirped, stepping back and putting up the umbrella to protect herself from the persistent drizzle and disappearing into the night. There was something familiar about the woman but he couldn't think what it could be.

Slightly disappointed that his caller had not been a work colleague, Vic closed the entrance door and returned to his flat. He went into the kitchen to throw away the outer wrapper in which the bottle of tablets had been delivered. Suddenly he became aware of how warm the flat had become. Placing the bottle on the work surface Vic took off the extra pullover and placed it on the back of the armchair in case he needed it again.

A cold draft seemed to blow past him as he returned to the kitchen and Vic made a mental note to check for places where such drafts could enter his flat. Picking up the bottle to read what the dosage notes stated, he was vaguely amused to see that the instructions were handwritten and not typed out. Nevertheless, the writing was very neat and clear:

'One tablet twice a day before meals.'

There were twenty-eight tablets in the bottle, enough for two weeks. These instructions suddenly reminded Vic he hadn't eaten since breakfast that morning. It had been his intention to visit one of the numerous cafés in the area for a good nosh up. However, he had little appetite, either for food, or venturing out in the miserable weather. After taking one of the tablets he looked to see what snack he could tempt himself with. Much to his surprise he decided to have one of the low fat microwave meals. He had only bought a selection of these on the off chance he might entertain a female friend who was counting the calories. Best be prepared for all eventualities, had been his plan. Checking the date, he noted the sell by date was only two weeks away. Not much chance of enticing anyone round here before then, he admitted.

The meal eaten, dishes and crockery washed up, Vic went back to check what was on television. After only about twenty minutes he decided there was nothing worth watching and he retired to his bed. Even though it was only just after nine o'clock and the road outside still had some traffic on it, Vic was fast asleep within ten minutes of getting into bed. A similar dream to the previous night's entered Vic's sleep state, with a few minor variations.

> This time he was standing next to the old man in the centre of the room where the fire had been. His companion was holding something shiny and seemed to be offering it to Vic before turning away from him. Next moment they were both in a well-lit room and this time they had been joined by the same attractive woman from the photos, dressed in a long white coat, similar to a doctor's. She turned and smiled at him while shaking her head in a negative motion. The scene changed.
>
> He was now standing by a river watching a group of children swimming and having fun. All except one boy who was sitting on a large rock by the water's edge. Looking at the faces of the children in the water he noted how familiar they looked. One looked like his ex-wife, Fiona. Another was Sergeant Proudfoot and yet another was the doctor from the hospital. Suddenly, as one, all the children in the water pointed at the large rock where the boy had been sitting, but he had now disappeared and in his place was a giant ball of fire which began rolling towards Vic. He turned to run and found himself

in a very deep canyon with no escape route. As he turned to face the flaming mass he looked at his hands and they were red raw once more and itched like anything. He began rubbing his hands on his coat…

"They will itch for a few days more, "the female voice said, moments after he woke up in his familiar surroundings. Vic turned and sat up slowly. Was that voice part of his dreams?

"At least you don't snore like some overweight men," the voice said.

Vic turned in that direction. A tall, rather thin woman was silhouetted against the doorway by the light from the passageway. Vic had always left one light on at night ever since he could remember.

"Who the bloody hell are you?" he snarled, sitting upright in the bed. He was about to throw off the bedclothes before suddenly remembering his total nakedness.

"There's no need to get up, we can talk as we are. You never did get used to wearing pyjamas did you, Vic?"

"I don't know if you realise it, lady, I'm a police officer and pyjamas or not, you've got five seconds to say what the hell you're doing in my flat, "Vic warned, about to throw off the bedclothes and parade himself in front of the female intruder.

"My God, if your mother heard you use such language in front of a lady she'd wash your mouth out with soap," she said in a mocking voice.

That was enough for Vic. To hear this person mimic his dear mother, who had only been dead for just over three years, galvanised him into action. Throwing the covers aside, Vic launched himself from the bed at the woman standing by the doorway. Despite the handicap of the recent ordeal he reached the door in good time but the woman had gone. He was about to run down the short hallway to look in other rooms when a voice called out from behind him, "You'll have to be a lot quicker than that to catch me, Vic. Put your dressing-gown on before you catch a cold."

Vic turned back into his room and turned on the light. She was standing in the far corner of the room, near the head of the bed. Now I've got her, he thought, she's trapped there.

"Whatever your game is, lady, you've picked the wrong bloke to play silly buggers with," he said, advancing towards her. He was only three paces away when she disappeared. Vic turned round once more at the sound of her voice,

"Can we call a halt to this chasing round? That wasn't my purpose for calling on you tonight, you can either get back into bed or put on some clothes before you add pneumonia to your list of problems," she said quietly.

"My only problem is you!" Vic snarled and took a pace forward. Once again the woman vanished. He stood there for a moment, wondering if this was really happening. Grabbing his dressing-gown off the back of the door Vic checked all the other rooms for any sign of the intruder, but he was alone. The entrance door to the flat was locked and bolted and all windows were firmly shut so it seemed impossible for anyone to have forced their way in or made an escape.

He walked back to his bedroom, scratching his head. She was sitting on the side of the bed and Vic made no move towards her but simply asked, "OK, I won't try and catch you but would you mind telling me what is going on?" And he went and sat in the easy chair at the furthest point from her.

"Before telling you who I am, do you believe in the hereafter?"she asked quietly.

"If you mean spirits and things, I didn't, but at this moment in time I'm not sure if this is a dream or what the hell is going on."

"Tut, tut, such language. Anyway, I'll ignore it for now. Vic, if I told you that I'm your sister, what would you say?"

"Now I know it's a dream! I never had a sister, I'm an only

child. Whoever, or whatever you are, get your facts right," he said angrily.

"I'm your twin sister, Vic. I died at birth," she said in a hushed voice.

Vic said nothing for a few moments. That simple statement made him shiver and he drew the dressing-gown closer over himself. He shook his head. "No, I was an only child. Mum would have told me of anything like that. Please, who are you really?" he asked almost pleadingly.

Before he realised it, she was kneeling at his side, her hand gently touching his arm.

"Mum wanted to tell you before she died but never knew how to bring the subject up. I promise you, Vic, I'm telling the truth and you will have firm proof of what I've said in no more than a week from now."

He looked at her features closely for the first time. She had the same fair hair, hazel eyes and a distinctive mole on the left nostril. She was about the same height as Vic but a lot thinner he noted as she stepped back to sit on the edge of the bed nearest to him.

After a few minutes' silence he said with a slightly croaky voice, "I'm still not certain of what's going on here, my logic tells me it's all a dream. But if it's not, why me? And why now?"

"Both questions have the same answers. You have to help bring to justice some very nasty people. But before that there are things you have to do for yourself. The attack on you has links with the past that need sorting out."

Vic interrupted. "But that's my job, I'm a police officer."

"Yes, we know. Look, I've told you enough for now and I'll return if you need me. You've had a luckier escape than you realise and rest will be an important part of your recovery. Before I do go, you must look after yourself a lot better. You need to lose weight pretty quickly. Hug the bedclothes, Vic," she said and leaned over and touched his forehead.

Her touch was soft and warm, but real. He blinked and she was gone. Her last words and action, more than anything, told him it wasn't a dream. The phrase, 'hug the bedclothes, Vic' was what his mother always said to him when he awoke from having a bad dream, and then she would touch his forehead and leave the room.

Through force of habit he made a quick tour of the flat to make sure all was secure, not sure in his mind if he wanted to find an unlocked door or window in order to give a logical explanation to these events. Vic was certain he wouldn't be able to sleep again that night and sat back down in the chair to try and rationalize his thoughts, but soon dozed off.

The chill in the room awoke him some time later, though it was still dark. Climbing back into bed he drifted off into a deep dreamless sleep.

4

The noise made by a Sunday morning car enthusiast revving up his engine eventually penetrated Vic's deep sleep and forced him to stir from his slumbers. Last night's events occupied his mind. Did he really have a ghostly visitor or had he suffered some sort of reaction to his ordeal?

Whether the event was real or not, the identity of the woman was the most difficult aspect for Vic to come to terms with. His father had died when he was only twelve years old and his mother had never even given a hint, let alone mention having lost a child at birth. The only other surviving relation he knew of was an elderly cousin of his mother's who had been in a nursing home for years. Vic wasn't even sure if she was still alive, or the address of the home.

But these things don't happen, he tried to convince himself. It must have been a dream, there was no other logical explanation. He never had a twin sister who died at birth, that was just too damn ridiculous to even begin to believe. As for those words, 'hug the bedclothes Vic', he must have been subconsciously thinking of his mother and her comforting words from when he was young and they had somehow drifted back into his thoughts.

He vaguely remembered something else about proof coming

in a few weeks. Well, from whoever or wherever, it would have to be pretty damn convincing for him to accept such proof, Vic decided. Maybe those tablets had some weird side effects. Well, he hadn't coughed since yesterday evening so there wasn't any point in taking any more of those.

After getting dressed and collecting the Sunday papers that had been delivered, Vic made himself scrambled egg for breakfast. Purely as an experiment he made his coffee without adding sugar and found the taste quite acceptable. The papers didn't contain any startling news, only the usual sensations about sport and film stars and the hunt for an heiress who had run off with her gardener. Since there was some pleasant late morning sunshine coming in through the lounge window, Vic put on a light jacket and went out for a stroll through the nearby park. After that he would call in his favourite pub for a lunchtime drink with the possibility of meeting a couple of his colleagues from the station. However, before leaving he double checked that all doors and windows were locked and secure.

Despite the sunshine a fresh wind took the edge off the temperature and he cut short his walk and went to the pub. He remembered the tablets and wondered if it was a wise thing to have alcohol as well. Oh well, he thought, one pint won't do any harm. However, the atmosphere was so smoky in the bar he had barely drunk a third of his pint before a bout of coughing forced him to leave and walk back home.

His coughing had subsided a little by the time he reached the flat; however, several people on the way gave him sympathetic looks at the sound of his discomfort. If the same thing was going to happen every time he entered a smoky room then his career in the police force could be in jeopardy considering the number of officers who smoked in his division.

Funny dreams or not, Vic felt he didn't have much choice but to continue taking the tablets. He went straight to the cupboard to retrieve the bottle and took one tablet. I don't suppose less than half a pint of beer can count as a meal, he thought. Just as long as the mixture of alcohol and the tablet didn't mean he would see little green men with three heads.

He was about to return the bottle to its place on the shelf in the medicine cupboard when something on the shelf above in a clear plastic bag caught his attention. He couldn't remember putting anything like that in the cupboard. Taking the bag out of the cupboard, to his puzzlement he found a gold-plated cigarette lighter inside. Even though it was inside the bag Vic could see that it wasn't a cheap one, neither was it new. There was some kind of inscription on one side of the lighter but it was too faint for Vic to read in the dim light of the bathroom. He walked into the lounge to have a better look.

Perhaps it was his police training, or maybe some sixth sense that told him not to remove the lighter from the bag. Whatever it was, Vic was convinced the lighter had a strong connection with his recent ordeal.

Peering closely through the bag at the lighter Vic could now see the writing more clearly. There were two letters, an R and an S, both in a very elaborate style. Below the letters were two numbers with a dash in-between. The numbers were 41 and 91. The numbers and letters were enclosed in a heart. All very pretty he thought, but how the hell did it get into my bathroom?

No visitors had called at the flat for at least six weeks, and of those who had, he couldn't think of anybody who owned such a lighter. The colleague who had collected his clothes the other night was one of a few who didn't smoke and would have no need of a lighter, let alone an apparently expensive one like this one. After racking his brain for a further ten minutes Vic returned the lighter to the bathroom cabinet and checked the freezer to see what he could have for his dinner.

Vic had enjoyed the meal the night before and wondered if a similar treat could be found. He was in luck. Having settled down to watch a favourite documentary on television Vic was a little annoyed when the phone rang and disturbed his viewing. Of all the people he least wanted to talk to that evening, Sergeant Proudfoot certainly knew when to pick his moments.

"Evening, Holland, sorry to disturb you, but Inspector Stevens wants to know if you can call in tomorrow to fill in some details of your little incident. He's suggesting 9.30 in the morning. Is that OK?"

Vic sighed resignedly, "Yes, that's OK with me, Sarge," and was about to hang up when Proudfoot's voice took on a mellower tone than Vic had ever heard before.

"How are you feeling in yourself, lad?"

This sudden show of kindness caught Vic unawares and he coughed a couple of times before replying and telling Proudfoot of his failed attempt to take some exercise earlier that day.

"Well you take it easy for a couple of days, you've had a nasty experience. I take exception to anyone laying a finger on my men, let alone trying to kill them," and he hung up before Vic could answer. Perhaps there was some degree of humanity in the old buzzard after all, Vic thought. Although he had never shown it before.

It was nearly midnight when he gave up his TV viewing for the night and took another tablet before going to bed. He hoped there would be no more unpleasant dreams.

However, his wish was not granted and he dreamt of food.

He was sitting down to one of his favourite meals, roast beef and Yorkshire pudding. The pudding was extra large and he started to cut it with his knife. But he couldn't cut it. He grabbed the pudding with both hands and tore it apart, spilling the remaining contents over the table. Inside the remains of the pudding was something solid in a plastic bag. He called for a waiter.

A young man came over and picked the bag up and Vic could see the gold lighter in the man's hand. However, it was the sight of the man's hand that disturbed Vic. It was badly burnt and deformed. Vic looked at his hands and they were the same.

He awoke in a sweat and quickly put on the bedside light to check his hands. Apart from itching a little, they were fine. Very soon he fell into a deep, dream-free sleep.

The previous day's sunshine had been replaced by a heavy drizzle and gusty wind. Vic wrapped himself in a large overcoat to gain protection from the elements and caught a bus to within a couple of streets from the police station. The bus was packed with people keen to escape the inclement weather and he had no choice but to sit next to an old man whose clothes reeked of stale tobacco. Vic could feel the irritation build up in his throat and even though the old man left the bus two stops later, the coughing started once more. It had only subsided a little by the time he entered his place of work.

A number of his colleagues stopped to ask after his welfare and one or two of the less sympathetic kind made comments about his lack of fitness.

"Ah, there you are, Holland. The inspector's waiting for you in Room 7. I also need to have a quick word with you before you leave," Sergeant Proudfoot announced in his usual brisk manner.

Inspector Stevens stood up to greet Vic as he entered the room and shook his hand warmly. "Glad to see you up and around again, Holland. How are you feeling after your ordeal?"

Vic coughed a couple of times before replying, "Apart from this blooming cough which starts up at the slightest hint of smoke I don't feel too bad thank you Sir"

"I'm sure the quacks will find something to clear it up. Anyway, sit down, Vic, I want to go over the events of the other night if you feel up to talking about things. No psychological after effects I trust?" enquired Stevens.

"No not really, Sir, just the odd daft dream that doesn't make much sense. I've been trying to think of any important facts about what happened but it's not worth much I'm afraid."

"Well, let's put your dreams to one side for the moment and concentrate on what you can remember about the events of that night," the inspector sighed. Were the stories he had heard about Holland's past beginning to affect his judgement? If so, Stevens didn't want him in his division.

Vic sensed that he had better be careful about what he said regarding his rescue so he limited his story to the bare details. He recounted first seeing the youths running from the shop, giving chase and being lured into the derelict building. The memory of the light being shone in his face suddenly reminded Vic of the names used by the youths.

"I'm sure one of them had the nickname of Torch, Sir, and he called his mate Keys or something like that," said Vic. He knew there was something else about one of the voices that was distinctive but what it was he couldn't be sure.

"Torch and Keys you say. I've heard those names before. Some of the local kids look on them as some kind of heroes. One's an arsonist while the other can break into almost anywhere; they break into premises, rifle through them for anything of value and then set fire to them to hide any evidence. From what I've heard, the one called Torch has got quite a vicious streak, so no one is willing to grass on him."

"I can vouch for that, Sir, who else would trap someone under a floor and then try and suffocate their victim?" Vic replied with a shudder at the memory.

"Why did they suddenly scarper from there?" Stevens asked.

"I remember hearing something fall, possibly some loose brickwork. Perhaps they thought the whole place was about to collapse around their ears," Vic presumed. Stevens nodded without saying anything, he was thinking of one possible place he could check out on these characters called Torch and Keys.

Vic had decided not to mention anything about his vague

recollections of his rescue, merely stating that he must have crawled out of the hole and collapsed near the doorway before being found.

"OK, Holland, if that's all you can think of for now we'll call it a day. Let me know if you come up with any other facts, not dreams," Stevens said in a dismissive voice.

Vic left the inspector to his thoughts and it was only as he walked back down the corridor that he realised nothing had been mentioned about his return to duty. He soon found out why. Sergeant Proudfoot led him into a small room behind the duty desk and closed the door, inviting Vic to sit down.

"You've had a pretty rough couple of days haven't you, lad? And it's not over yet, I'm afraid." He held up a silencing hand as he continued, "In view of what's happened and partly because of your general fitness, the inspector wants your next medical test to be brought forward to the end of next month."

"That's only six weeks away, Sarge, it doesn't give me much time to sort myself out. I know my weight has got a bit out of control lately but I'm sure I could get through the medical if I had the time to get fit again," Vic protested.

"Well six weeks is all you've got or you can kiss the force goodbye Holland."

"How the hell am I supposed to do it in that time? I'd have to run a marathon nearly every day and I've got no chance of doing that even without this bloody cough." And as if to emphasise the point Vic started coughing once more.

When he had stopped, Proudfoot spoke. "Ever since you arrived here I didn't think you were up to making a mark in this force and I think you know that. But if you really want to prove me wrong I'm willing to offer you some advice if you'll listen."

Vic nodded and Proudfoot continued, "You came here nearly five months ago just wanting to hide away from your past, with no interest in making a fresh start. So you were given all the mundane jobs and you didn't complain, you just accepted things as they were. If you want to get on around here you have to push yourself to the front more often, not hide in the background. That may have worked in a country beat, but it doesn't work here, lad. Now if you want to have one last crack at staying in the police I can point you in the direction of someone who can at least try and get you in condition. Do you want to give it a go?"

"Of course I do, Sergeant. I don't know any other work. What have I got to do?" asked Vic, reluctant to disagree with his superior's analysis of his previous problems.

"Right, first of all, you're on sick leave until the medical, so go to your doctor to sign on and ask about a crash diet. Then visit the new sports centre in Walker Street and ask to speak to a bloke called Ernie Newsham. He's an ex-colleague of mine and former PE instructor. If anyone can get you fit he can. One more thing before you go. The lady who dialled 999 was asking after you yesterday. It might not be a bad idea to visit her to say thank you, she lives across the road from where you were rescued, at number 42, and her name is Jenny Potter."

"I'll do that, Sarge and thanks for the advice." Vic got up to leave the room.

"I'll be quite happy for you to prove me wrong, Holland, but I'll bet a tenner you won't make it," was Proudfoot's final remark as Vic left the station.

Well, if he ever needed an incentive to get fit the sergeant had just given him one. And he would enjoy taking that tenner off that pompous old sod.

5

The curtains in the bay window of the terraced house moved slightly as the occupant peered outside to check the identity of her caller.

Ms Jenny Potter rarely had visitors and was a very cautious person who never answered the door without first having a good look at her callers. The well-built young man now standing at her door was not someone she had seen in the neighbourhood before. Having caught the slight movement of the curtains Vic turned round so that the person could have a good look at him. The curtains closed again and Vic looked around at the shell of the building that had almost become his final resting place. Even in the weak October sunshine there was a foreboding look about the place. The memory of his escape sent a cold shiver down his spine.

A group of council workmen were using a cherry picker to repair the faulty street light next to where Vic had nearly succumbed to the attack on him. Pity that light wasn't working the other night, he mused to himself.

He had decided to visit the lady immediately after leaving the police station, just in case she could throw some light on the events of that night but he didn't hold out much hope. It was nearly two minutes before the door was finally opened, with just enough room for Ms Potter to ask Vic what he wanted.

"My name is Vic Holland, Ms Potter. I am the man who was rescued from the derelict building across the road last Thursday night. I've come to say thank you for calling out the rescue services."

"How did you know it was me who phoned them?" she asked suspiciously.

"My colleagues at the police station told me that you made enquiries about my welfare yesterday. I'm a police officer as well," Vic said, hoping to reassure the cautious occupant.

The door closed slightly and the sound of a security chain being released could be heard, followed by the door being flung open.

"Don't just stand there young man, come in, come in!"

Vic did as he was told and followed the sprightly lady inside as she led him into the lounge area and shooed two cats off the settee where they had been dozing. Vic was invited to sit down.

"I'll be back in a moment, just wait there while I make a pot of tea, Mr Holland," Ms Potter said as she left the room with the two cats in her wake.

"You don't have to go to any trouble, Ms Potter, I just called to say thank you for what you did the other night," Vic stated, hoping he would not be detained for too long. Jenny took no notice of his protests and went into her kitchen.

With a policeman's eye for detail Vic looked around the room. It was tidy, with everything seemingly in its place and not a speck of dust on any of the surfaces. There was no modern furniture in the room, even the television set in the corner must have been at least ten years old. He suddenly became aware of something rubbing against one of his legs.

The smaller of the two cats, a ginger tom, was sitting next to him, rubbing its head on his shin. He turned to stroke it and the cat stood on its hind legs as if it was about to climb onto his lap.

However, before it could do so, the other cat arrived in the room and hissed a warning. The first cat lowered itself back onto all fours and ran into a corner of the room and watched from safety.

The second cat took up the position of its smaller cousin but rather than go through the rubbing routine, it jumped straight onto Vic's lap without an invite and settled down, purring softly. Vic dared not move for fear of disturbing the animal. Moments later, Ms Potter arrived with a tray adorned with teapot, two cups and a plate of biscuits. She placed the tray on a small table beside an armchair and proceeded to pour the tea.

"I see that Fish has accepted you as a friend, Mr Holland. I always say that if a cat adopts anyone as a friend then they must be a nice person. I'm sorry, I seem to have forgotten the sugar. Do you have sugar in your tea?"

Rather than put her to any trouble Vic shook his head. "Your other cat was about to make himself at home on my lap before this one chased him away. I take it this is the leader?"

"Oh yes. Fish lets little Biscuit know who is boss, but they usually get on well together. Now tell me, what were you doing in Mr Stockwell's old shop?" she asked, passing him a china cup filled to the brim. She clapped her hands and the cat seemed to understand the signal, jumped off Vic's lap and went to lie at his mistress's feet.

Vic described the bare facts of the night's events, trying not to alarm his host with too many lurid details. She sat quietly without showing any emotion throughout his story and before finishing Vic asked what had alerted her to the danger he had been in.

"I was just about to settle down to watch a documentary on the television that I had been looking forward to seeing for ages. I'd fed the cats and made my cup of cocoa and was sitting in this chair when the lights flickered and went out. I thought it was a power cut, we have a lot around here, so I went to the front window to check if everywhere else was in darkness. But it wasn't, I was the only one! I looked around for a few moments and it was then I saw the smoke rising from the old shop. Seconds later two people ran out of there and disappeared down the road. I went to phone 999 and as I did so, the lights came back on in the house. Very strange it was."

"Also very lucky for me you did look out of your window or I might not be here to have this cup of tea with you," Vic answered.

"It was a pity I wasn't here the night Mr Stockwell's shop burnt down or he might still be here as well," said Ms Potter, her eyes moistening slightly.

Vic could see some past memory had upset his host, nevertheless he could not resist probing further. "I thought there had been a fire there before, what exactly happened?"

She sat quietly for a few moments before regaining her composure. "I wasn't here the night it happened, my sister had gone into hospital in Ipswich and I went to visit her. By the time I'd left the hospital the last bus had gone so I stayed the night at my niece's house.

"I'd only been speaking to Mr Stockwell that morning and he was in good spirits. He was due to visit his granddaughter in Canada the following week. Anyway, it seems a fire started in the room below his flat and he died in his bed, apparently overcome by the smoke. The fire brigade said he must have left a lighted cigar downstairs and that started the fire, but I don't believe that story," she ended defiantly, wiping a tear from her eyes.

"Why do you say that?" Vic asked, not wishing to upset her but at the same time an overwhelming curiosity made him persist.

"Mr Stockwell was a very careful man. He told me he never smoked downstairs because that was his old workroom when he was a pharmacist and he wouldn't dream of contaminating that area with smoke. Even though he gave up his work shortly after his wife died four years earlier. Someone else started that fire, Mr Holland, but no one will believe me," she said with surprising venom.

"I think I believe you, Ms Potter, but can you answer me just a couple more questions. How long ago did this happen, and can you describe Mr Stockwell to me?" Vic was keener to know the answer to the second question but wanted to hide the fact for the moment. Ms Potter finished her tea before answering,

"It happened almost two years to the day of your accident and I've been pestering the council to pull down the remains of the building ever since because I knew it was dangerous. As for Mr Stockwell, he was rather tall but quite thin. And very strong for his build and age. He wore horn-rimmed glasses. I'm sorry, Mr Holland, I don't want to carry on this conversation any further, it's too upsetting for me. If you would like to come back another time I might be able to tell you more."

Vic could see there was no point in pushing for any more answers so he passed the cup back to his host and rose to leave. As she opened the front door to let him out, she made one more comment that had Vic thinking all the way home.

"As well as being a wonderful pharmacist Mr Stockwell had other skills not given to him by man and I'm sure he won't rest in peace until the mystery of his death is solved."

Vic took one last look at the burnt-out building and wondered if it was pure chance he had been drawn there on that night. He would have gone over to have a closer look but glanced at his watch and suddenly remembered the appointment he had made at the doctor's surgery.

Fortunately the surgery had been busy and all appointments were running late. He had to endure twenty minutes of sitting amongst the usual batch of sneezing and coughing patients before it was his turn. Although after five minutes of Dr Bowden's critical appraisal of him, Vic wondered if it had been worth the wait.

"If you're a typical example of today's policeman it's no

wonder there's so much crime around. First of all, you need to lose at least two stone in weight and cut out those cigarettes before they kill you, man."

"I don't smoke, Doctor, that must be the smoke I inhaled in the accident that's causing my breathlessness."

Bowden grunted. "Well in that case what tablets did the hospital give you to clear it up, they don't seem to be having much effect."

Vic said he couldn't remember but promised to bring one for the doctor to look at the next day. The comment earned a second grunt from Bowden. "Well I'll tell you this for free, young man. I'm on the medical panel that will be checking on your fitness and at the moment you haven't got a cat in hell's chance of getting through it. On the other hand, if you feel up to the challenge you'd better start by going on a diet right now. Call in to see the nurse and she will give you a list of food to steer clear of for the time being and she can also check your weight."

Fortunately the nurse was free and after weighing Vic and taking his blood pressure she gave him a list of the things he should eat and those to avoid. A quick glance depressed him even more, most of the banned food was the type he had lived on for the past six months. Ironically nearly all the good food was what Fiona had fed him on during their marriage. At least some benefit had been gained during their relationship.

"If you do the right exercises and stick to that list you should lose a couple of pounds a week to start with but don't expect miracles. Losing weight and keeping it off is a long-term job."

With the nurse's words ringing in his ears Vic cancelled the intended visit to the pub and called at the sports centre to have a talk with Proudfoot's ex-colleague. Even though he was in his early fifties Ernie Newsham looked fitter than most men twenty years younger. He took Vic into the café adjoining the large swimming pool and they sat down with their coffee.

"I've already had a phone call from Peter explaining what

your problem is. How much weight are you supposed to lose before your medical, Vic?" Newsham asked in a fatherly tone.

"The doctor reckons at least two stone."

Newsham shook his head slowly. "That's a bit much to lose in just six weeks and stay fit enough for the medical. Let's set a target of twenty pounds and anything above that will be a bonus. Can you swim?" he asked.

"I was a late starter and I'm a bit rusty. It must be at least a year since I had a decent swim," Vic mused.

"By the time I've finished with you, lad, there will be fins on your back. I'll also set up a series of exercises on the cardiovascular equipment in the gym to release the boredom of swimming fifty lengths a day."

Vic's mouth dropped open at the thought of such a routine. Newsham continued, "Let's get one thing straight from the beginning, Vic. I'll help you as much as I can but it's really down to you. If you've got any doubts about doing this, say so now because I don't want to waste my time if you aren't fully committed."

Vic thought for a moment before replying. "It's mostly my fault I've got into this state and if I want to stay in the police, which I most definitely do, then it won't be for the lack of trying on my part."

"OK, Vic. Meet me here at eight o'clock tomorrow morning and you can make a start. I don't expect you to swim fifty lengths straight off, but you need to reach that target within a week. While you're building up to that you can have a few sessions in the steam room, followed by the Finnish sauna and finishing with the cold plunge pool each day. Has the doctor put you on a diet?"

Vic nodded and they shook hands before he went home. The first thing he had to do was find his swimming trunks and make sure they fitted! Only just.

For the next two weeks he went through the rigours of the

fitness routine Ernie had set up for him. His first session did little to encourage him in his endeavours. Vic had only managed ten lengths of the pool on that first visit. A grim-faced Newsham watched from the balcony at his pupil and realised it wasn't going to be plain sailing in achieving their target. By the time he'd completed two circuits of the equipment in the gym, spent two sessions of ten minutes in the steam room followed by a quick dip in the icy cold plunge pool Vic couldn't believe how unfit he had become.

"I've seen fitter corpses in the morgue than you, lad, you're really going to have to push yourself a lot harder than today. Tomorrow I expect twenty lengths from you, and if you don't then you'll have to come back in the evening to try again," was Newsham's parting comment.

It took him three visits to the pool and gymnasium to reach Ernie's first target, but with each session he slowly started to feel the benefit of his new regime. It wasn't until the start of the second week Vic achieved Ernie's target of fifty lengths of the pool. Even so, his instructor grudgingly accepted that Vic was putting in his best effort as his weight started to come down faster than both had dared to hope.

6

On the morning Vic achieved the fifty lengths target set by Ernie, he returned home for his breakfast which was now also part of his fitness plan, along with the rest of his diet. He had to admit the food was tasting much better than he had expected and grudgingly accepted that the fry-ups he had got into the habit of eating almost on a daily basis had been part of his weight problem.

While taking a tablet before the meal he suddenly remembered the cigarette lighter and its initials, R S. He finished his breakfast and retrieved the lighter from the cupboard to examine it once more. This lighter was a vital clue, how he came by it was not important at the moment, but he felt there was a link between his ordeal and events from the past. And he knew who might have the answer.

Jenny Potter was brushing away the fallen leaves from the path outside her front door. She stopped as Vic approached and greeted him with a smile. "I thought you might have come back sooner but here you are now."

She went indoors, inviting him to follow. Taking his place on the settee Vic was joined by the younger of the two cats who sprung onto his lap and settled down, purring loudly. Ms Potter entered the room with her customary tray and placed it on the coffee table. She turned and addressed the cat, "Yes Biscuit, you know Fish is out of the house at the moment so make the most of your comforts."

Biscuit purred even louder.

"I hope this isn't an inconvenient time for me to call, Ms Potter but I remembered something that might have an important bearing on events of the other night," Vic began.

"Young man, do you always talk in that manner? Anyone could tell you're a policeman just by the way you speak," she chided, but with a hint of a smile creeping onto her features. Vic coughed and felt his face colour slightly. To try and hide his embarrassment he put his hand in his jacket pocket and brought out the lighter, still in its clear plastic cover.

On seeing what Vic held in his hand, Jenny Potter's expression changed completely. Her face went an ashen colour and she had to grasp the teapot with both hands before it dropped on the floor. Very shakily the teapot was returned to its place on the tray, both cups only half filled. She stared at Vic, motioning to him to pass the lighter to her. He said quietly, "Please don't take it out of the cover Ms Potter, it may have some fingerprints on it."

She seemed not to notice what he had said, merely holding the covered lighter in her hand, while staring back at her guest. After a few moments she looked down at the item in her hand, turned it over and her eyes welled up with tears. A little choking cry was forced out of her throat. Almost immediately, Biscuit bounded off Vic's lap and ran to his mistress's side. He was joined, as if by magic, by his older companion and both cats gently pawed at the hem of Jenny's dress. Vic rose to his feet and went over to pour the rest of the tea into the cups. He offered one to his host but she waved it away. Instead she took out a lace handkerchief and dabbed her eyes. It was another two minutes before she spoke in a husky voice, "Please tell me exactly how you came to have this in your possession. I must have the truth, young man. No lies or half truths."

Her tone reminded Vic of the first time he had given evidence in court. The judge that day had been equally serious in his request for the truth and Vic had been as honest as he had ever been. Now was just such a time, but if he didn't know the full story himself how could he convince this lady that the strange facts he was about to relate were true? As he began Vic noticed that both cats had now turned around and were also staring at him, as if waiting for his story,

"It's a little difficult, Ms Potter, because I don't really know the full facts myself but I'll do the best I can."

She nodded her head and Vic continued to relate the circumstances of how he had found the lighter in his cupboard. He finished lamely, "I'm sorry but I can't offer any rational explanation of how the lighter ended up in my flat."

Far from being dismayed by his story Jenny sat forward in her chair and asked eagerly, "Think very carefully Mr Holland before you answer this question. Did you notice anything unusual in the room before or after you found the lighter?"

Vic thought for a moment and was about to shake his head when something sprang to the forefront of his thoughts. Before he could stop himself the words blurted out. "As I went into the kitchen I felt a draft as if someone or something had dashed past me. There were no windows or doors open so it couldn't have been a draft."

Instead of dismissing his words as unimportant, Jenny leant even further forward and asked if that was the first time such an occurrence had taken place. Vic told her about the repeated feelings of coldness that had seemed to follow him around the room on his return from hospital. He concluded that was the result of the after effects of his accident. Jenny Potter would not hear of such a thing. "No, no. You have had a presence in your flat who must have put the lighter in your cupboard. Tell me, do you believe in ghosts Victor?"

That was the first time in ages since anyone had used his proper name in full and Vic had to smile. "To be perfectly honest, no, I don't believe in ghosts."

"Then can you offer any other explanation as to how the lighter came to be in your cupboard if you didn't put it there yourself?"

Vic could not, but seeing his host had regained her composure he tried to divert the attention from his apparent scepticism. "What significance does that lighter have to you Ms Potter?"

"Before I answer I'll go and make a fresh pot of tea, this one has gone too cold to drink." With that comment she stood up, placed the lighter in her cardigan pocket, picked up the tray and made her way out to the kitchen with both cats trailing close behind.

While he waited for her return Vic tried to think of a logical and rational answer to explain how the lighter had turned up. Having already mulled this over for the past several days he had to admit there still wasn't a rational one that sprang to mind.

Jenny returned with the tray and proceeded to pour the tea and handed him a cup before she sat down and spoke. She had wiped away her tears and spoke in a clear calm voice, "Before I answer your question please allow me to apologise for my little outburst just now. It came as quite a shock to see that lighter after so long."

She took a couple of sips from her cup and began her story, holding the lighter firmly in one hand. "The letters on this lighter shows it belongs to Robin Stockwell, the retired pharmacist whose shop you nearly perished in. The two numbers below the initials, 41 and 91, signify the number of years Mr Stockwell and his wife, Stella, were married. The initials could also stand for Robin and Stella. You see, Mr Holland, Stella gave her husband this gold-plated lighter on their golden wedding anniversary. I was there when she presented the lighter to him. It was quite sad really because she died less than six months later from cancer that not even Robin knew about."

She wiped a tear from the corner of one eye before continuing. "Let me take you back many years before then, in order to try and help you understand more fully about events at the shop. Robin and Stella met in the late thirties when she was sent over here from Germany to live. Her parents felt it would be safer in this country because of the anti-Jewish feelings at the time. Stella's mother was Jewish and her father was German so they stayed behind with Stella's two younger brothers. She lost all contact with them shortly before war broke out and never heard from them again and neither did she find out what happened to her family, but I think we can all guess.

"Robin had just qualified as a pharmacist and they married in 1941, moved into the shop across the road and opened it up as a chemist's. Even though the war had started Robin was exempted from being called up at first, partly because of his profession but he also had a slight limp. He joined the medical corps in 1942 but never left these shores. I was told that Stella was given a bit of a hard time by some locals because of her origins when Robin was away but their attitudes changed completely in later years. One or two others were also a little guarded about Stella for another reason but I'll explain later.

"A few years after the war ended their only child, a girl called Patricia was born. I was six months younger than her, my family moved in here two years later and Patricia and I became the best of friends. I spent a lot of time in their flat above the shop and Robin and Stella treated me like a member of their family. They were also very supportive to me and my mother when my father died in the early sixties.

"In the late sixties the big pharmaceutical companies began to push their mass-produced drugs but Robin would have nothing to do with them. He continued to make up all his medicines and tablets in the same way as he had always done. He lost some business at first but within less than a year these customers began to drift back. He carried on working in the same way he knew best right up to when he was forced to retire. But there was another side to Robin and Stella that gave locals reason to visit them."

She paused to finish her tea, placed it on the tray and sat slightly forward in her chair as if to emphasise a point. "I mentioned that some people were suspicious of Stella during the war. As you probably know, there was no NHS at that time and many people didn't go to visit a doctor when they needed treatment. It appears that soon after Robin joined the medical corps a local lady called in the shop for something to put on a swelling on her knee. Stella had to tell the woman that Robin had gone away and that she couldn't make up anything to put on the swelling as she wasn't qualified. Stella had a good idea what to do as she often helped Robin. But if word got around that she was making up any lotions or anything like that, someone would have called the police sooner or later.

"Instead, Stella asked if she could have a look at the swelling on the woman's knee. Having been in agony with this problem for several days she agreed. Stella invited her to sit down and knelt in front of her to examine the knee. As well as being badly swollen, there was a boil on the edge of the knee. Stella gently placed both hands around the area of the problem. She carried on in this position for several minutes, then got up and told the woman to come back in a couple of days. The very next day the woman called to see Stella again to show that the swelling and the pain had gone overnight and there was no sign of the boil. Stella just nodded and smiled. I know that story is true, Mr Holland, that woman was my mother.

"Word got around and there was soon a number of regular callers at Stella's back door. All kinds of ailments from migraine to a frozen shoulder, lower back problems to women's complaints were all part of her clients' reasons for visiting Stella. But as I mentioned earlier, there were a few people who tried to cause trouble for her. You see, if certain people can't understand or don't want to believe what is happening they immediately think there are evil practices taking place. A few threatening letters were pushed through her letterbox and she actually had an old man throw stones at her one day and calling her all kinds of unpleasant names. In the end a friendly policeman called on her and advised Stella to refrain from her healing sessions for a while or someone might do something silly. Despite this advice she carried on but in a more discreet manner.

"When Robin returned from the war and found out about these events he was a little worried. However, Stella assured him there were no evil doings or intent and after he attended one of her healing sessions he was won over. In fact Robin discovered he also had the gift of healing but not to the same extent or power as his wife. But Robin was much more skilled in making up his medicines and lotions and he concentrated on them and allowed Stella to carry on with her healing when it was required. Talking of Robin's lotions, I can remember one day when I was playing with Patricia in the flat and I scalded myself with a pan of boiling water. It was just before Easter and we were boiling some eggs to decorate them. Somehow or other the pan of water was knocked over and the water spilt down my dress. I started screaming and ran down the stairs to come home to my mother. Robin must have heard my cries and met me coming down. Realising what must have happened, he tore off my dress and carried me into the back room where he mixed up his prescriptions. My lower body and legs were bright red and already beginning to blister. Robin then took down a large bottle of white cream and spread it over the burns. I must have passed out from the pain because I don't remember anything else. When I came to, I was covered in this white cream but

I could feel no pain. My mother was sitting next to me. I was eight years old at the time."

Vic felt a strange sensation on the back of his neck. What had the doctor in the hospital said about his burns? An image of a tall thin man standing in some kind of working area planted itself firmly in his mind. The man turned to face Vic, who could see his features quite clearly now.

"Could you describe Mr Stockwell to me?" Vic asked, trying to keep focused on the image.

"Well, he was quite tall, at least six foot three I would think. His body always looked as if it needed feeding but he was very strong. Strangely enough, even though he was thin in the body, he had quite a chubby face. This would have looked odd on most men but not Robin. He wore horn-rimmed spectacles and had a receding hairline. What hair he did have, was grey and always collar length. Stella always tried to get him to cut it shorter but that was one thing he refused to do for her. Why did you want to know?" she enquired, and suddenly noticed that Vic's face had paled as she spoke.

The description could not have been closer to the image that had flashed across his mind even if she could have reproduced it for him in the form of a photograph. A thought suddenly came to him. "Did you mention earlier that Mr Stockwell had a slight limp?"

"Yes, he injured his right hip when he was a small boy. Do you want me to carry on? You've gone a little pale."

"Please do," he said, taking a bite out of his third biscuit.

"Well anyway, where was I, oh yes. We borrowed a dress from Patricia and I went home and mother insisted I go to bed to rest, even though she had wanted to take me to the doctor's to make sure I was going to be alright. But Mr Stockwell had assured her there would be no need. When I awoke the next morning there was no sign of the burns and I could feel no pain! Whatever was in that cream performed a little miracle, Mr Holland.

"Patricia and I grew up together, went to the same school and carried on nearly like sisters. Then Patricia met this man and they eventually got married, although Stella was not really happy with her choice of husband. Unfortunately she was proved right some years later when he was killed while trying to rob a bank in France. By this time their daughter, Natalie had been born. Patricia was so devastated by her husband's double life she emigrated to Canada with Natalie after her sixth birthday. Robin and Stella visited them a couple of times but I never saw either of them again because Patricia died about eight years ago. She had remarried over in Canada and as far as I know Natalie is living with her stepfather.

"I mentioned at the beginning that Stella gave this lighter to Robin on their golden wedding anniversary shortly before she died. Robin had one vice in his life, he loved to smoke those thin cigars during the evening when he was relaxing in a small room at the back of the shop. Stella wouldn't allow him to smoke anywhere else in the building and he promised not to. And do you know, Mr Holland, he stayed true to her memory by sticking to that promise right up to when he died. I know that because I used to go and clean the flat for him after Stella died."

"When did he retire and give up his business?" Vic asked.

"He gave up the pharmacy business on his seventy-fifth birthday, mainly because he had difficulty in obtaining some of the ingredients for making up his own medicines. Also, a new bigger chemist opened up a few streets away and nearly all his customers started going there. So instead he concentrated on selling herbal remedies, but that wasn't very profitable. It's a pity people's memories only seem to last as long as their pockets are empty of money. There aren't many families around here who didn't get credit from Robin at one time or another. After Stella died he lost interest in the shop and closed it within six months. One or two of the older folk would call on him from time to time when they had a small twinge that they didn't want to bother the doctor with. He still had that healing gift right up to the end, as one or two around here will testify. However, his visitors got less and less apart from myself and a couple of others from the local spiritualist church. I cooked a Sunday roast for him every week and took it over to his flat."

Vic glanced at his watch and was surprised to see their conversation had gone on for nearly two hours. He would have to leave soon but he didn't want to be rude and walk out before she finished her story. He tried to bring the story to a conclusion by asking, "I remember you saying yesterday that Mr Stockwell died in a fire in his flat; do you have any idea what was supposed to have happened?"

"The coroner said that Robin must have been smoking downstairs and forgot to put his cigar out, and that started the fire. Whatever Robin was, you could never call him careless. Every night when he finished smoking he would hold the stub of the cigar under the cold tap before putting it in the waste bin. He would then leave his packet of cigars and the lighter on the table by the ashtray. Someone else started that fire Mr Holland!" she finished defiantly.

"You can't go saying things like that without proof, Ms Potter. Do you know if he had any enemies?" Vic asked, hoping his host wouldn't start making any wild accusations.

"No, not Robin. Except perhaps some of the local yobs who sometimes threw stones at the shop windows and broke a few of them. But you couldn't call them enemies. I have some problems with their litter and bad language but I couldn't call them enemies. No, that's the young people of today I'm afraid."

"You don't have children of your own?"

"No, Mr Holland. I never married, I was too busy taking care of my mother after she developed chronic asthma until she died eleven years ago."

"I'm sorry, I didn't mean to intrude."

She smiled. "Don't worry Mr Holland, I'm not the frustrated spinster most people round here think I am. Before she got married, Patricia and I had more boyfriends than I care to mention. Oh, I've just remembered something else. About five weeks before the fire Robin told me of two youths who called on him one night. One of them had badly burnt his hand, so bad Robin said the skin had melted and his fingers seemed to be stuck together. Robin put some of his cream on the burn and said he couldn't do anything else and told them to go to the hospital straight away or the boy could lose his hand. He hadn't seen them before or after that night."

Jenny hesitated before continuing, seeming to want to pluck up courage before speaking. "Robin did say something to me on the last Sunday before he died. He had tried to advise Mr Newsham, the man who runs the Leisure Centre, to be wary of those two youths as they were, well, in Robin's word 'not good news'. Robin was quite surprised when Mr Newsham became very angry and wouldn't hear any bad words against those two, and left their meeting. The next time they met Mr Newsham was his usual pleasant self and apologised for his manner and tried to explain that those youths were from broken homes and everyone seemed to pre-judge them and they were good lads really."

"And what was Robin's reaction to that comment?"

"He said he decided to keep his own counsel and didn't pursue the matter, but still had his reservations about them."

Vic made a mental note to check out the date and details of the original fire at the shop. He could also make enquiries with the casualty department at the hospital if they had any records of treating severe burns to a youth's hand at about that time.

"Didn't you mention that to the police at the time of the fire?" he asked.

She remained silent for a few moments, unsure as to whether this policeman would treat her words with the same disdain as his predecessors had done. Finally she spoke. "I told them of what I knew about Mr Stockwell's habits and his regular safety checks before going to bed. At first they accepted what I said as the truth.

"The night after the fire I had a very vivid dream of Robin asleep in his bed and someone standing over him with a pillow in their hands. Then I woke up with the sensation of being suffocated. I was completely breathless for a few minutes, it felt just like an asthma attack. Before you say the same as your colleagues, Mr Holland, I know my mother was a chronic asthmatic and I could have inherited it from her. However, I never had a trace of asthma before or since and my doctor can confirm that fact. The next night I woke up in the early hours and I swear to you now, the figure of Robin Stockwell was standing at the foot of my bed!" And to emphasise her final remark she banged her fist on the arm of the chair, so firmly both cats jumped up in surprise. Her face had also gone a very bright red and she suddenly burst into tears at the memory.

Vic went over to Jenny and knelt by her side, offering his handkerchief. She accepted it and dabbed her eyes several times. Gradually her composure returned and she waved Vic to sit back in his chair, assuring him that she felt better and wanted to continue.

"I'm very sorry about this, I've not been able to talk to anyone who I felt would understand. Yet even though we've just met, there's something about you that says to me that you are willing to listen."

He felt flattered by her words and was intrigued by these past events. "Did you tell the police about the dream and sighting of Mr Stockwell?"

She nodded. "As soon as I mentioned seeing Robin in my bedroom, everything else I had told the police didn't seem to matter. I was just another of those silly women who attend the local spooks club as it's called. They mean the spiritualist church, and I've only been about a dozen times in my life.

"There was an inquest and the coroner recorded a verdict of accidental death. I was too upset to attend and even if I had, I'm not sure I would have had the courage to speak out, or if anyone would have believed me. Sergeant Proudfoot said that without proper evidence they couldn't have come to any other verdict."

"Did you mention the lighter to the police?"

"Yes, but because the roof fell in during the fire it was assumed it had been lost in the rubble. But now that you've got the lighter, it can only have been taken by the person who started the fire," she finished triumphantly.

"That's certainly possible, Ms Potter, but it might be difficult to prove it was arson on just the discovery of the lighter. It also gives me a little problem of how it came into my possession. I'm not completely sure myself," he sighed.

Once more he was reminded of his mother's stern tones: "You're forgetting one thing Victor. We're talking about murder as well as arson. Isn't Robin entitled to justice?"

"I can have the lighter checked for prints and make some enquiries regarding the information you've given me, but I can't make any promises. If there's nothing else you can tell me about the lighter or anything to do with the shop fire I'll have to go now, but whatever happens I'll keep you informed," and he reached over to retrieve the lighter from Jenny.

She clung onto it for a few moments longer, reluctant to be parted from the memories she cherished but at the same time it saddened her. "What will happen to this once the police have finished with it?" She asked, finally handing the item to Vic.

"That's really up to any relatives of Mr Stockwell. Did you say something about a granddaughter in America?"

"Canada," she corrected. He nodded in apology. As Vic rose to leave, her final question caught him unprepared: "Do you have any surviving relatives?"

Without thinking he replied, "Only a cousin of my mother's. I was an only child and both my parents are dead."

The moment he finished speaking two things happened in the same instant. He felt that same cold feeling that had plagued him in his flat and both cats jumped up together as if linked by an invisible cord. Their hairs stood on end and they ran out of the room as if a large ferocious animal was on their tails. Jenny followed their movements and then looked back at Vic. She put one hand to her mouth and sat back in her chair, her eyes fixed on something just beyond his right shoulder. He turned to look round but there was nothing to be seen. The cold feeling had also disappeared. His look of puzzlement brought a smile to Jenny's face.

"Do you know what has happened, Victor?"

He shook his head and she continued, "I've just seen my first spirit. It was a young lady, about your height, but much slimmer. She had a mark on her nose, just like yours. Would that be your mother when she was younger?"

Vic nodded purely through reflex, not wishing to contemplate the idea that he had not simply been dreaming the other night after all. As much as he trusted Jenny Potter, there was no way he wanted to discuss even the remotest possibility of him being the sole survivor of twins. No, Jenny's mind was playing tricks. Their talk had aroused feelings of remorse about the past within the sad woman and her imagination had taken over. As for the cats, well, probably some noise or other must have frightened them.

The denial was written quite plainly over Vic's face and although Jenny knew it would serve no purpose in pressing the matter any further for the moment, she would have to pick her moment carefully.

"Thanks for the tea and biscuits, Ms Potter, as soon as there's any news I'll let you know," Vic said as casually as he could manage. Perhaps he should have a talk with his doctor about the attacks of the shivers that kept recurring.

After watching her guest close the garden gate, Jenny closed the front door and turned to the cats who were now sitting at the bottom of the stairs "We know what we saw, don't we boys?"

7

By the time he reached the police station Vic had conjured up what he thought was a reasonable story of how the lighter had come into his possession. As long as Proudfoot didn't become too inquisitive he should get away with his story.

The sergeant was on his lunch break and Vic found him enjoying his pipe in the rest room. Fortunately no one else was present. Rather than show his hand right away Vic casually asked his superior about the original fire at the chemist's shop. Proudfoot looked thoughtful before finally speaking. "Pretty straightforward case really. Old man asleep upstairs, having forgotten to put out his last smoke of the evening. I believe the forensic people found evidence of the fire starting in his lounge downstairs and it took hold and spread through the rest of the building. What didn't help was the fact he kept some of the chemicals he had used when he was still practising. Highly inflammable some of it was so the fire brigade said, that's why nearly everything went up in smoke.

"I remember seeing some bottles of the stuff when I called on him after he complained of kids breaking some windows in his place. The council were informed but before they could take any action regarding removal of those substances the fire happened. The Coroner's verdict was accidental death."

"Didn't one of his neighbours dispute that?" Vic asked.

The sergeant gave him a curious glance. "Been talking to the Potter woman have you? Yes, she came up with some cock and bull story about the old man being suffocated, or so her dreams led her to believe. Let's say that could have occurred, we didn't have a shred of proof. The body was too badly burnt and crushed, the roof fell in. I can't understand why the council hasn't pulled the rest of the ruin down. It certainly would have saved you a lot of bother."

Before showing the lighter, Vic asked, "Supposing Jenny Potter was on the right track, maybe someone was trying to cover up a break-in or something?"

Proudfoot shook his head. "Nothing worth stealing in that shop, he'd retired years before. No lad, it was just one of life's nasty accidents waiting for the unwary. Yes, Ms Potter swore he never left his cigars burning, that he was very careful, but we all have our lapses, even me. Look, chatting to you and my pipe's gone out. Oh well, no peace for the wicked, and no comment from you."

Vic produced the lighter, still in its plastic cover. "Can I offer you a light Sarge?" and passed it over to Proudfoot, who eyed him suspiciously.

"You don't smoke, Holland, so what's so special about this lighter?" He turned it over in his hand and noticed the markings on one side. "What does RS stand for?"

"Robin Stockwell, the pharmacist who died in the fire."

Proudfoot put down the lighter and pipe on the coffee table in front of him. He noted the way his colleague sat slightly forward in his chair, a sure sign that a person was either nervous or keen to impart some information. So let him have his say. "I haven't got much of my break left, so rather than me interrupt you at every point and waste time, tell me what you know. Or perhaps more likely, what you think you know."

The last remark stung Vic; he wondered if Proudfoot was

the person he should be talking to. There was little choice. "I found the lighter in my coat pocket after returning home from hospital. How it got there, I can only guess. Perhaps one of the rescue team found it on the floor of the building and thought it was mine and put it in one of my pockets.

"Anyway, as you suggested I called on Ms Potter to thank her for alerting the fire brigade about the incident. She told me about the first fire in the shop and how she thought Stockwell was murdered. That was before I showed her the lighter, which she positively identified as belonging to the old man. She clearly remembers Stockwell's wife giving it to him on their golden wedding anniversary because she was at the party. His wife died shortly after so it was a priceless memento he kept with him at all times.

"You mentioned a few minutes ago that the roof fell in and no evidence of anything suspicious taking place. Then the only person who could have got hold of the lighter was someone being in the building shortly before the fire. Apart from Stockwell it could only have been the arsonist. Look at the condition of it, you'd expect at least some marks if it had been in the building when it collapsed. If the lighter was put in my pocket the other night, it must have been dropped by the same person who started the first fire."

Sergeant Proudfoot was silent as he inspected the lighter; when he finally spoke Vic felt the anger building up inside him. "If what you say is true then we're looking for a murderer who tries to commit the same crime in the same place twice. However, in all my years as a serving police officer, I can't recall there being a case of someone attending a rescue and removing evidence without first checking how it came to be there. You'll have to come up with a better story than that to convince me, let alone a judge and jury."

"Are you saying I concocted this story with the help of Ms Potter? An old man who bent over backwards to help others is killed in dodgy circumstances, and I nearly get choked to death in the same place. And what happens? Nothing, that's what! OK, if you think the story I told about how the lighter came to be in my possession sounds barmy, then try this reason for size, it's even more bizarre." As he finished speaking, Vic felt his face burning bright red. His raised voice also started another coughing fit which he thought he had seen the last of.

Proudfoot fetched him a glass of water and sat down to listen to Vic's new account. After calming down he went on to relate the circumstances of how the lighter had been discovered in the cupboard in his flat, giving the minimum of details.

"Yes, I'm not sure which story I find dafter to be honest. Forget how you found the lighter, unless you can prove Stockwell had it right up to the time of the fire. There's always the possibility, however remote, that he lost this lighter and it was picked up by someone else. That's the line any defence lawyer worth his salt would take."

"How come it ended up in my flat? Nobody else has access and that lighter was not in the cupboard on Saturday night when I last looked in there. I found it in that same plastic bag and that's where it's stayed ever since. Check for fingerprints and DNA if you want, neither I nor Jenny Potter have handled it but someone put the lighter in the bag for a reason, and I don't think it was for purposes of hygiene."

Proudfoot sighed. "I'll speak to the inspector first and let him decide if this has any bearing on your attack. But my advice to you is not to mention your theory about the death of Stockwell to anyone else unless you've got much stronger proof to link it with your incident. Now I've gone over my break time so let's leave things as they are for the moment. Oh, I nearly forgot something. Some woman from a nursing home in Southend rang yesterday asking if you were the same Vic Holland who used to live in Stretchborough some years back. When I confirmed that was the case she said she would send some papers to you concerning a relative of yours. You should receive them in the next few days. Anyway I'm late for my shift so remember what I said."

Vic had mixed feelings about his talk with Sergeant Proudfoot, on one hand the lighter would be checked for fingerprints etc. and this might help in identifying a culprit. On the negative side, had he given Proudfoot further ammunition to get rid of him? After all, could someone who believes a cigarette lighter simply materialised from nowhere and ends up in his flat be of sound mind to carry on his duties as a policeman? His apparent support of Jenny Potter in her insistence that Stockwell was murdered wouldn't go down too well with some people either. Well sod them, I'm not letting this drop just to climb the popularity ladder, he decided. They'll rig the medical so that I fail anyway.

Going back home to ponder over events wouldn't help much either. Putting himself through the rigours of another workout would take his mind off the mystery of the lighter. Taking a slight detour on his way to the sports centre for another torture session with Ernie Newsham he called at the doctor's surgery to leave a sample of the tablets given to him by the chemist. Fortunately Dr Bowden was not available, a bonus in Vic's mind, as this spared him having to sit through another lecture by the medic.

Whether it was the opportunity to take out his frustrations and anger at the lack of understanding shown by Proudfoot or the determination to succeed in his fitness battle, Vic made a significant improvement in his performance by completing the fifty lengths of the pool in his best time to date. Even Newsham showed a semblance of being impressed. "If you can show that much improvement in a few hours there might be hope for you yet. Better that performance tomorrow and I'll accept this was no fluke. Come on, I'll treat you to an orange juice."

They sat in a quiet corner of the coffee shop, but rather than be forced into talking about his past, Vic asked his trainer why he had left the force. Ernie Newsham said nothing for a few moments, he looked in Vic's direction but his gaze seemed to be on some distant object. For one fleeting moment there was a look of resentment, even anger, but it disappeared just as quickly and he gave a little smile as he started speaking,

"Believe it or not, it was on health grounds, about ten years ago. I suffered a back injury after the patrol car me and Pete Proudfoot were in turned over during an emergency response. I was nearly crippled for life and that lucky sod only had cuts and bruises," he said, his smile being replaced by a light frown.

"You had to leave on health grounds? But you're as fit, if not fitter, than most of the blokes in the division. How come?" enquired a puzzled Vic.

"After the accident, I spent five weeks in hospital. I had a crushed vertebrae in my neck and two punctured discs in my lower back. Oh, a smashed kneecap and numerous other minor injuries thrown in for good measure. At one point, the quacks were considering sending me to Stoke Mandeville but I told them to sod off. I wasn't ready to be strapped into no bloody wheelchair. All I needed was an operation to put things back into place and I would have made it.

"It took several months, but I pushed myself as hard as I dared in the circumstances to get fit enough to return to duty. I nearly damn well did it too! Except for my neck and back, I was A1. But the bloody quacks refused to operate on my spine, they said the risk was too great. They were scared an operation would fail and I'd end up crippled and sue them for negligence. I offered to accept all responsibility, but they wouldn't play along.

"'I'll show you bastards, I said to them. I was absolutely desperate. I can't remember how many second opinions I had, all with the same result. Sorry, Mr Newsham, we can't help you, they said. Then the last consultant I saw mentioned something quite out of the blue. After giving me the usual garbage he said as I was leaving, 'I hope you find your miracle, because that's what it will take'. That got me thinking. Some years earlier a colleague's wife had been introduced to a faith healer as they were known at the time. She had cancer, but it didn't work out and she died. Anyway I pestered my mate until he told me the name of this healer. In the end he told me but said I was wasting my time. I didn't care, I was ready to give anything a try. The police force was my life, I didn't know anything else. The first two healers I visited were bloody useless, and the third wasn't much better. But he gave me a name of a lady who might agree to see me.

"The first time I met this woman, there was, I can only describe it as a glow about her. She was dynamite! I only went about six times but by then I knew my spine was cured. And to prove it I had X-rays taken at my own expense and even visited the last consultant I'd been seen by. He didn't believe it at first either, test after test that bloody bloke put me through. In the end he finally admitted defeat and told me, 'All my medical training and experience tells me this couldn't happen, but it has and I don't know how. Mr Newsham, you found your miracle worker.' And he was one hundred per cent right!"

"Who is this woman?" Vic asked casually, finishing the remains of his orange juice. He had expected coming here would have given him some peace from unexplained happenings. Newsham's answer shattered his reasoning.

"Oh, she died a few years ago, her name was Stella Stockwell."

With his mouth half open, empty glass suspended in mid air, Vic sat in this frozen pose for what seemed like an age before the cry of a disciplined child nearby broke the spell and he heard Newsham's repeated question. "I said, are you OK? I thought you were trying to catch flies until you went as white as a sheet. You look as if you're in need of something stronger than orange juice, hang on while I get you a whisky."

Placing the empty glass on the table, Vic raised his hand in a sign of refusal. A dozen questions ran through his mind, each answer would raise another dozen. He started with the most obvious. "You must have known her husband then?"

"Knew Robin? Course I did. I was a regular visitor to their flat before and after Stella died. In fact I was probably the last person to see him alive."

"How come?"

"I gave him a lift home from the meeting we were both attending as I did on every occasion, why are you so interested anyway?" Newsham was becoming a little wary of Vic's probing.

"One more question before I tell you what's on my mind. Do you know if he still had his cigarette lighter with him that night?"

"The one Stella gave him? You're damn right he did, it never left his side. Except at night, when he left it by a photo of him and Stella on the mantelpiece in his lounge. OK, now I've answered your questions, you tell me where's this all leading to."

Vic hesitated and looked at his watch. What he had to say would take some time and he didn't feel comfortable bringing up the subject in such an open venue. "I've come across something that has a lot to do with Robin Stockwell's death and I don't want to discuss it in public. Can we meet somewhere more private, maybe my place?"

"You mention Robin's lighter, I take it that's the connection?"

Vic nodded and Newsham pretended to pick something from behind a fingernail before speaking again. "OK, give me your address and I'll call round tonight if that's convenient."

A relieved Vic took out a pen and wrote the details on the back of a serviette before asking one more favour, "I'd appreciate it if you didn't mention this conversation to Sergeant Proudfoot. See you about eight."

Newsham nodded and watched Vic leave, thinking back to the time when he was just as keen an officer. He also remembered that despite his return to fitness after Stella's help, he still wasn't allowed to have his old job back. So he had embarked on another career outside the law.

***

"This better be worth it, lad, I've put back a dinner appointment with a young lady to be here," Newsham said when Vic met him at the main door and led him upstairs to the flat.

It took Vic about twenty minutes to tell the story of the events surrounding the lighter's appearance and all the details Jenny Potter had told him. However, as with Jenny, he made no mention of his own dreams. For the time being he didn't feel confident enough to divulge such personal secrets to people he had only known for a few days. In fact he couldn't think of anyone he could confide in about such matters.

Ernie Newsham sat quietly throughout, watching Vic closely for any hint of deviation from his story. He had heard the Potter claims before and had been sympathetic towards them. After taking Robin Stockwell home that fateful night, Ernie had gone home to pick up his luggage and driven down to Heathrow Airport. He had flown out to Australia that morning and not heard about the fire until his return. By that time the inquest had been held and without very strong evidence there was no chance of re-opening the inquiry. He asked Vic, "What's your theory on the fire?"

"The only solution I can come up with is that someone broke into the building, possibly with burglary in mind. They searched around, eventually ending upstairs in his bedroom. Perhaps he awoke and found whoever it was in his house. Or they woke him up to make him tell them where his valuables could be found. Maybe they simply smothered Robin and started the fire to cover their tracks.

"The lighter was taken by the thieves and either it was the

same ones who attacked me who committed the first crime and dropped the lighter, or it was passed onto someone else and they were the ones who beat me up. I don't really know if there was one or more persons involved in both events, and whether they're the same person or people. But that is not my concern at the moment.

"My main point is that if you can confirm Robin Stockwell had that lighter in his possession when you left him, for it to reappear now in such good condition points to the probability it was taken from him by the thief or thieves who started that fire which killed him."

Vic sat back, wondering if his theory was watertight. Ernie kept him waiting for what seemed like an age before replying, "Yes as I told you earlier, Robin had his lighter with him inside the flat when I left. But as a copper you should know that the theory on its own is not enough to charge anyone with murder. Is there anything else you can remember about those yobs who beat you up that night?"

Vic got up and walked to the window and looked out, appearing as if trying to recall some detail from that night that could have some significance. He turned around to face his guest and watched closely for any reaction to his next comment. "Two nicknames were mentioned, Torch and Keys, would those fit any of your clients at the Leisure Centre? You must get to know some of them pretty well."

A flush of anger swept across Ernie's face and was gone in an instant but Vic had noticed the change. Ernie spoke in clipped, measured tones. "Vic, most of those who attend the Centre and youth club are good kids. There are one or two who come from, let's say, difficult backgrounds, and they get blamed for everything from dropped litter to armed robbery that takes place across this county. I know them and can vouch for every last one of them.

"Look, I know the meaning of such nicknames and if I

thought any person attending my Centre was involved in Robin's death or the attack on you, believe me, I'd hang them out to dry. I'm an ex-copper, Vic, and I wouldn't have any such person set foot in my place."

Vic simply nodded but he had an uneasy feeling about Ernie's defence of his clientele. How could he be so sure of their whereabouts 24/7?

Ernie continued, "There is some riff-raff in this town but don't try to blame my lads for your attack, I bet they're from much further afield."

"Well, one of them had a northern accent, Yorkshire, I'll bet," Vic said casually, watching for any further reaction, but this time Ernie's features remained blank.

Ernie glanced at his watch and stood up. "I'm sorry, lad, but I can't keep this lady waiting any longer. Try and think back to that night of the incident and break down the events into smaller parts and see what you come up with. You never know what might pop out of your subconscious when you least expect it. I'll see you at the pool tomorrow morning. 'Night!"

Vic showed his guest out and as he climbed the stairs back to his flat the throbbing pain returned to his hands, but this time a lot stronger than at any time since the fire. Sod what old Doc Bowden said about the tablets, they worked for him and that was good enough reason for Vic. Opening the cupboard door in the kitchen and reaching for the bottle, Vic was surprised to find that there was only a single tablet left. He was convinced there should have been more than one.

The throbbing in his hands brought his thoughts back to the present and he swallowed the final tablet with some water. He was due to see the GP again for the results of his analysis, hopefully tonight was an exception and the pain would disappear for good. He returned to the living-room and sat in the chair recently occupied by Ernie and tried to relax, waiting for the discomfort in his hands to subside. The throbbing slowly gave way to a feeling of rapidly increasing heat on the palms of both hands, yet the colour stayed the same.

The tablet didn't seem to be having any effect, perhaps one wasn't going to be enough this time. Not being able to bear the discomfort any longer Vic went back to the kitchen to find some other painkillers he knew were there. After swallowing two of the tablets he wrapped both hands in two kitchen towels that he first dampened under the cold water tap. By the time he sat back down the discomfort had become more bearable and Vic closed his eyes in an effort to relax.

Vague shapes danced before his eyes, they seemed familiar, yet unrecognizable as being totally human. Each one came closer in turn. Features cleared and became more distinguishable as the shapes came closer. The first one was Ernie, but not completely. The head and torso were the ex-policeman's, but his legs had been replaced by what at first appeared to be a pram. No, not a pram, a wheelchair.

Ernie disappeared and was replaced by a much younger man, more likely a youth. Vic couldn't make out his features but his left hand and forearm were engulfed in flames. This apparition also disappeared and a woman took his place and glided towards him. Her features were also difficult to make out and there didn't appear to be anything unusual about her. In an instant the picture changed and Vic knew the woman was his former wife, Fiona. Her face was racked with pain and a metal object stuck out of her chest. Before disappearing she spoke, "Look at your hands, Vic, my Dutch treat, you're one of us now. A cripple..."

The continuous ringing of the phone brought Vic back to the present with a bang. He was bathed in perspiration yet he shivered uncontrollably. The phone rang another four times before he removed one of the towels from his hands and picked it up and gave his number. Ernie's voice boomed back at him, "What the heck are you playing at, Vic? You should have been down here thirty minutes ago. If you don't get a move on I won't have time to introduce you to a friend of mine. You are coming in for your session aren't you?"

Removing the towel from his left hand Vic glanced at his watch. It read 9.40 am. That was impossible, he thought, no way had he slept all night. But it was true. Once more Ernie's voice cut through his thoughts. "Look sunshine, if you took too much out of yourself yesterday, just say so and we'll just call your improvement a fluke. I need to know now, are you coming in right now or not?" There was a slight irritation in his voice so that Vic felt he was under obligation to answer in the positive.

"I'll have a quick shower and be there in thirty minutes," he replied.

"Forget the shower and make it fifteen," was the curt reply and the phone was slammed down before Vic could object.

A few things that appeared in his dream didn't make sense to Vic at first. He obviously knew his wife and Ernie but who was the boy? Ernie was still very much alive and his wife was dead, but what of the boy, was he dead or alive?

He was also a little surprised that the graphic reminder of the circumstances surrounding his wife's violent death didn't fill him with grief as it had done so many times in the past. Even though they had been so much in love before and during the early years of their marriage, these feelings meant nothing after Vic discovered Fiona had been cheating on him for several months prior to her death. And he had been the one to find her body and that of her lover.

A call had come through on his patrol car radio requesting any available unit to attend a road traffic accident. The report had merely stated that a heavy dumper truck had apparently run off the road and smashed into a parked car. Vic responded to the request and as he approached the location a man and a woman waved him down. Another man was sitting on a grass verge with his head in his hands. Vic could clearly see some slight damage to the lorry but there was no sign of the car it was supposed to have run into. The couple were vaguely familiar to him, he recognised the woman as the widow of the school caretaker.

"Hello, Mrs Roberts, did you report the accident, and who's that chap sitting over there?" Vic asked as the couple approached.

"No, it was my brother who phoned in and that man is the lorry driver. I don't think he's hurt but he seems to be in shock."

The brother nodded to confirm this statement. Vic looked around for the other vehicle that was supposedly involved in the accident. Anticipating Vic's next question the man pointed to his left-hand side and said, "The car was pushed through those railings and over the edge onto the railway line. I had a quick look but couldn't see anyone moving around inside and then I dialled 999."

Vic's heart missed a beat, was that railway line still in use? He looked at his watch and sighed with relief as he remembered it was only a branch line and the last train would have passed this point over an hour ago. He walked over to the lorry driver and tried to ask him what he knew but the man didn't even look at Vic, he sat in the same statuesque position, head in hands and staring at the ground. There would be little point in trying to ask the driver any more questions, besides there could be someone trapped in the car in need of his help.

Before going to investigate Vic retrieved a warning triangle from the boot of his car and ran back up the road to warn approaching vehicles of the danger ahead. He left instructions with the man to tell the fire brigade when they arrived where he was, collected a torch from his car and began the slippery descent towards the railway line below to check if there were any occupants inside.

It had been raining earlier that evening, making the grass slightly greasy and slippery underfoot, brambles tugged at the legs of his uniform and he was aware that the slope ended with a six foot vertical drop onto gravel and chippings by the side of the track. He scanned the area with his torch to find the safest route to go down. He found the edge of the drop just as the first sound of the approaching fire engines wailed in the still night air. Dropping down onto the gravel and shining his torch around once more to find his way in the total darkness, Vic found the car on its roof, straddling one of the two railway lines.

The lorry must have been travelling at some speed to have pushed the car so far out onto the track, Vic surmised, as there were no signs of the car rolling down the bank he had just scrambled down. The damage to the rear of the vehicle seemed to confirm these thoughts. The boot of the car had been crumpled up so much it had been crushed into the main compartment of the car and the rear window was missing. There was no sign of petrol leaking from the tank but its pungent smell filled the air. As he walked round the back of the upturned vehicle he stood on a mangled piece of metal and shone his torch on the number plate by his feet and froze. He knew the number as well as anyone else would know the registration number of their partner's car. Vic blinked several times, hoping he had misread the number but he knew it was a forlorn hope.

The sound of a vehicle applying its air brakes on the road above broke the spell and Vic made his way around the car to the driver's door. The angle at which the slim tanned arm hanging through the open window seemed to be beckoning him forward.

Vic steeled himself for what he was about to discover. He had attended numerous road traffic accidents in his five years in the force and each one had its own unique features. Stepping over the metal railway line Vic knelt down by the open driver's window and shone his torch inside. For a brief moment his hopes rose as he shone the torch on Fiona's face. She seemed to be sleeping as her eyes were closed. He reached out to stroke her face and feel for the signs of a pulse in her neck. There was none and Vic realised why. The head was at a rakish angle to the rest of her body. He didn't need any doctor to tell him that her neck was broken. He slumped down onto the gravel and took her hand and held it gently in both of his own. But something puzzled him. Why was her blouse open to the waist, exposing her to the cold night air? He never heard the shouts of the firemen as three of them scrambled down the ladder they had placed against the side of the bank. Their leader tapped Vic on the shoulder, not recognizing him in the dark. "We'll take over now, mate, you've done all you can."

Vic spoke quietly without turning. "It's Fiona, Dave. She's gone."

Dave, the First Officer of the local part-time retained fire crew knelt by his friend and put a hand on his shoulder. Vic and Fiona had been guests at a family wedding on the previous weekend. Many people had commented how they looked like the perfect couple. As the two friends knelt together another fireman came over and whispered something in his colleague's ear. He gave brief instructions to the fireman and turned to Vic. "Vic, we've got work to do, there's someone else trapped inside and he's still alive."

It took a few moments for the message to register with Vic. Who could this person be? He suddenly remembered Fiona's open blouse and picked up his torch so that he could see to cover her up from prying eyes. Even in death she had the right to some dignity. What he saw next made him recoil in horror. Apart from the open blouse his wife was completely naked. A piece of metal also protruded from the left side of her body, possibly a piece from the iron fence the car had crashed through on its way down to the track. Vic pushed his friend's consoling hand away, staggered to the side of the track and was violently sick. Dave picked up Vic's torch and looked inside the car and realised the significance of the discovery. Both occupants of the vehicle were near naked.

Two more firemen climbed down the ladder carrying cutting

equipment on their backs. They were followed moments later by another police officer. Dave quickly took the policeman to one side and told him what they had discovered, suggesting to him to try and take Vic away from the scene. Without warning, Vic pushed past them both and began ascending the ladder to the road above. Dave motioned to the policeman to follow his colleague. "Keep an eye on him, he's not thinking straight and liable to do something daft."

The warning was prophetic: as Vic reached the top of the ladder he walked past Mrs Roberts and her brother as if they didn't exist and headed straight for the lorry driver. Even if he had been prepared for it the driver wouldn't have stood much chance of warding off the first blow. Even though he was a big man, the punch knocked him to the floor. Fortunately, before a second blow could be delivered Vic's colleague caught up with him and pulled him back. "Leave him alone, Vic, it's not all his fault. If you want to have a go at someone pick on that bloke in the car down there."

Vic ignored the remark and tried to aim another blow at the frightened lorry driver but was pulled back by the other officer. Vic snapped. With a yell, he turned on his companion and tried to hit and kick at the same time. The woman's brother came to his assistance and moments later a second fire engine arrived on the scene to find one civilian and a policeman fighting with another police officer. Vic was restrained and finally calmed down and allowed himself to be driven back to the police station.

The lorry driver was later prosecuted for driving under the influence of alcohol and having defective brakes on his vehicle. A verdict of accidental death was passed at Fiona's inquest, and the man who had been with her would be confined to a wheelchair for the rest of his life due to the extent of his injuries.

Fiona had been acting as a bereavement counsellor and the man had been introduced to her after his wife had died from cancer. Their affair had blossomed from that point and had been continuing for several months.

Despite the circumstances Vic had been a little fortunate that the lorry driver had not pressed charges for assault against him, or he could have been kicked out of the police force. Instead he was given a long period of compassionate leave and transferred to another force. That was how he had arrived in Clapfield.

The cold rain stung his face as he jogged all the way to meet Ernie Newsham. Vic had to admit he was feeling a lot fitter than he had done for a long time, perhaps there was a better than even chance of passing the medical after all.

Ernie was waiting for him in the changing room "About time too! In the pool and start off with thirty lengths, I'll be timing you so give it your best effort. Then I want you to meet someone."

Vic was tempted to ask who the mystery person could be but knew Ernie wouldn't tell him until he was good and ready. Nothing could be gained by annoying him any further.

An elderly couple were the only other occupants of the pool so Vic had a good clear run at complying with Ernie's instructions and he was just completing his sixteenth length of the pool when he spotted his tormentor approaching the edge of the pool with another person. Vic was swimming free style so he only caught glimpses of the pair every fourth stroke when he was facing in their direction. At first, all Vic could be certain of was that the second person was most definitely female.

She was nearly as tall as Ernie but there the similarity ended. The tracksuit she wore added grace to her athletic stature. The light brown hair fell to her shoulders and hid her face from Vic's view. So intent was he in trying to catch a glimpse of her features that he failed to notice the direction in which he was now swimming. Instead of splashing through water his forward hand suddenly hit soft flesh and a yell of protest from the elderly man whose rear end Vic had inadvertently slapped brought his attention back to the present. Vic mumbled an apology and turned to swim the other way.

However, the yell from the elderly man had achieved the desired effect as far as Vic was concerned because Ernie and the woman turned to see the cause of the commotion. He could now see her face in full profile. And what he saw nearly made him swallow water. His mind flashed back to the dream of a few nights past and the third of the three photographs he vividly remembered. In the photograph she had been wearing a graduation gown and an elderly gentleman was standing just behind her left shoulder.

"If you've finished assaulting my other customers and drinking the water you can have a breather and come and meet Natalie," Ernie said with a little sarcasm.

Vic mumbled an apology to his fellow swimmers and swam to the edge of the pool while still keeping his gaze firmly on Natalie. Was his mind playing tricks on him again or had he really seen a photograph of her before? He stayed in the water at the edge of the pool, unable to take his eyes off the attractive woman.

Natalie was aware of Vic's constant gaze and felt a little uneasy. She had got quite used to being stared at by male admirers, after all, that was part of the fun of being a good looker. Men could stare as much as they liked, as long as they didn't try and touch. And if the uninvited did try their luck, she was quite capable of looking after herself. But there was something different about the way Vic was staring at her that made her feel uneasy. He seemed to be looking at her as if she was some kind of ghost.

Ernie had also noticed how much attention Vic seemed to be paying to Natalie and deliberately stood in front of her to obscure his view. He called out, "You were making good time until the last length, have a breather for two more minutes then do another ten lengths. We'll be watching from upstairs on the balcony so you won't get distracted."

He turned around, took Natalie's arm and steered her towards the stairs leading to the balcony and cafeteria. Vic watched them walk away and tried to clear his mind. Had she been the woman in the photograph? And who was the old man? Why had they been in his dreams? Ernie's voice boomed out from the balcony. "I said two minutes rest, not two hours. Make that forty lengths and get moving. I'll have the stopwatch on you. Remember you need to at least equal yesterday's time. Now get moving!"

Vic responded with a wave, I'll show that sod and his girlfriend. By the time he had completed the forty lengths of the pool Vic was blowing pretty hard and he hadn't noticed Ernie standing at the edge of the pool, this time by himself.

"Pretty good, you knocked eight seconds off your last time. Do you want to do any gym work as well?"

"I think I'll give that a miss for now. My hands were pretty sore after you left last night, perhaps I overdid things yesterday," Vic replied.

"Fair enough, have a shower and then join Natalie and me in the café for a light lunch. And this time, Vic, try and keep your eyes in their sockets or Natalie will mistake you for just another lecherous sod."

Having thought that the young woman might have left, the news that they would be having lunch together gave Vic fresh energy. He hauled himself from the pool and headed for the showers, keen to have a closer look at Ernie's companion.

They were deep in conversation and didn't seem to acknowledge his arrival for several seconds until Natalie looked up and gave him a slightly shy smile. Ernie made the introductions. "Natalie, this is Vic Holland, a serving policeman who is in the habit of getting himself into hot water. Vic, I'd like you to meet Natalie Jardine who is visiting the area for a short while."

They shook hands and Vic sat down, trying hard not to stare at her but failing miserably. Natalie broke the ice. "Do you always give new acquaintances such close scrutiny or is that just the policeman in you?" she asked, now with more of a mischievous smile lighting up her features. The Canadian accent was clear, but not overpowering.

Vic felt his face glow a little and blustered back, "Sorry, I didn't mean to stare but you reminded me of someone I saw in a photograph."

She liked the idea of Vic looking and, no doubt, feeling flustered. "OK, I've heard most of the good chat up lines so what's your angle?"

Ernie sat back and watched the two of them, amused at the exchange and Vic's apparent vulnerability. Vic's answer changed the relaxed atmosphere into one of tension and mistrust. "Sorry, it's not a chat up line, it's just that I'm sure I've seen a photograph of you in a graduation gown with an older man, perhaps your grandfather, standing just behind you."

The change to Natalie's features was instantaneous. Her colour went from a rosy colour to pale grey and back to bright red in seconds. She sat with her mouth half open, not sure if she had heard Vic correctly. Even Ernie looked taken aback by Vic's comment. Natalie recovered her composure, but spoke in measured tones that did not try to hide the fact she was hurt by the remark. "There is a photo of my graduation day about eighteen months ago but how you would have seen it beats me. And for the record, there was no one else in that picture. Ernie, can you point me towards the bathroom, I need to pay a visit."

She stood up quickly and walked off in the direction that Ernie indicated. Neither man spoke until she was out of earshot and then Ernie rounded on Vic. "I didn't put you down as an insensitive bastard but you know how to land a low blow. Why did you come up with such a stupid remark as that?"

Vic was confused. He thought he was just making small talk with Natalie. Even in the short time he had been in her company he felt as if they had known each other for years. "What did I say wrong? She does remind me of someone I swear I saw in a photograph. What's the big deal?"

Ernie looked livid and Vic started to feel uncomfortable.

"Firstly, lad, as she said, she did graduate eighteen months ago but I'm the only one who has seen that photo outside of Canada. Secondly, there was definitely no one else in the picture. Tell me, Vic, do you know who she is?"

Vic thought for a few moments and shook his head.

Ernie continued, "You said the other person you claim was with her was her grandfather, or someone of that age. Vic, her grandfather was Robin Stockwell. And Natalie graduated in Toronto State University one week after Robin died here in England. Natalie was asking about the circumstances of his death while you were swimming."

Vic sat forward and covered his face with both hands. Why the hell did he blurt out the mention of the picture only moments after meeting Natalie. You only saw it in a dream you stupid prat. Try explaining that to her and you will make a lasting impression. But not one to be proud of, sunshine.

"Are you alright, lad?" Ernie asked as his colleague sat in a trance-like state. Vic appeared not to hear him so Ernie leaned over and tapped him on the shoulder and repeated his question.

"Apart from making myself look like a complete idiot and being totally insensitive to someone else's feelings I think I am OK. But right now I wish I hadn't bothered coming here after last night's events."

"What's that supposed to mean and how does that justify what you said to Natalie?"

Vic got up from his chair and after checking there was

nobody within listening range he said quietly, "Ernie, I can't justify it right now and I'm truly sorry for upsetting her by saying what I did. I've been having some weird dreams lately and odd things have been happening to me. I think some of it's down to the tablets the doctor gave me to help after the accident. I'm seeing him this afternoon. Apologise to Natalie for me and I hope we can meet again before she leaves. If I'm up to it, I would like to have another shorter session in the pool and gym later this afternoon, so I'll see you then."

Ernie grabbed Vic's wrist and spoke very slowly. "Vic, there is one thing you should know about Natalie. She told me she's a Black Belt, Second Dan in Aikido and she is quite capable of knocking six bells out of you if you pushed her too far!"

Vic pulled his arm away from Ernie's grip and said, "Maybe that's what I deserve right now."

Before Ernie could respond Vic turned around and almost ran for the exit, he couldn't face Natalie right now, his embarrassment was too great.

Natalie returned to the table only moments later and asked where Vic was. Ernie merely said that he was late for a medical appointment and had apologised if he had offended her.

"I don't accept second-hand apologies so he'll have to do better than that. Anyway forget him for now, you said you would show me where my mother's parents used to live. And I'd like to meet this Jenny Potter you mentioned last night. Is that OK?"

She had recovered her composure and spoken to Ernie with such a disarming smile, he could only nod in compliance.

8

"Mr Holland, I won't beat around the bush so tell me the truth, where did you get this tablet from? And before you try and give me a load of waffle let me remind you that as a serving police officer you could be in very hot water for handling dangerous substances like these. So the truth please!"

Vic sat dumbfounded for a few moments, what was the old duffer on about, dangerous substances? These were the same tablets prescribed by the hospital and delivered by the courier from the pharmacist's.

Vic pointed this out to Dr Bowden who sighed deeply, got up from his chair and went to a large shelf to retrieve an old battered book. He sat down and searched through the book until he found the page he was looking for. He spoke in a soft but deliberate manner. "Victor, I sent that tablet you left for analysis. The laboratory rang back and asked me if I was trying to play funny buggers with them."

Seeing Vic's puzzled look he continued, "They found traces of substances that haven't been used by the pharmaceutical industry for nearly twenty years. In fact, they were more commonly used when chemists used to make up some of their own drugs, but as I said that practice has long gone. Mind you, at least in those days there was less chance of side effects from some of those medicines, not like today."

Vic started to get a strange sense of foreboding about what Bowden was telling him now; coupled with previous events things were taking a turn towards areas that he really didn't want to contemplate.

"Did you hear what I said?" Bowden's voice sounded its irritable self once more.

"Sorry, no I didn't," Vic mumbled.

"Apart from your lack of concentration which you've just demonstrated, are there any other side effects you've been suffering since taking these tablets?" the doctor asked.

Not wanting to give anything but the minimum of details until he had time to think more clearly about this turn of events, Vic said as convincingly as possible, "No, Doctor, apart from feeling a bit sleepy from time to time."

"No hallucinations or funny dreams?" Bowden asked.

A sense of relief descended on Vic. So it was the tablets that caused his imagination to play havoc with him after all. But he wasn't about to admit this to Bowden. "No, nothing like that at all, Doctor. In fact I haven't slept so well for ages," Vic said with a smile.

Bowden frowned. "Hmm, according to the lab report those tablets were strong enough to have you climbing the bedroom walls at the very least. I'm not entirely convinced by your answer so I want a blood test taken before you leave. And in the meantime I'll contact the chemist where you got them from and see what they have to say. If you've nothing else to add, see the nurse on the way out and give a blood sample. I'll be in touch when the results come through in about four days. Oh, I've left a prescription for some tablets at the desk, legal ones this time."

"Nothing to add, Doctor, and thanks."

Bowden didn't even look up as Vic left the room, he was too busy reading the old book he had opened.

After seeing the nurse to give his blood sample and collecting his new prescription Vic took a small detour back to the pharmacist's. He wanted to hear the full explanation about the mix-up with his tablets first hand. He had to wait for about fifteen minutes before the pharmacy dispenser was free to talk to him; fortunately it was the same person he had left the original hospital prescription with several days earlier. He asked if they could talk privately as it was a rather delicate matter and was led into a small waiting room.

"I have just spoken to Dr Bowden, Mr Holland, and I'm as mystified as you must be about the mix-up and can only apologise most profusely for what has happened. I personally handed your tablets to the courier to deliver to you."

Vic remembered their conversation from that previous time. "I thought you said you would personally deliver them after closing the shop, but it was a young lady who brought them to me."

"Yes I know, Mr Holland, but I had an urgent sample to deliver to the hospital so I rang the courier dispensing team to deliver my late prescriptions. Although I have to admit I have never seen that young lady they sent before."

Vic frowned. "Have you checked her out with this courier team and can you describe her to me?"

"Not yet, I will do so as soon as we have finished talking. As for her description, she was about your height, slim build and with some kind of mark on her nose, not dissimilar to the one you have."

At this last remark Vic closed his eyes briefly and shook his head, which caused the pharmacist to enquire, "Are you alright, Mr Holland, is it someone you know?"

"No, no it's nothing. If you can check things out and let me know when I collect the correct prescription later on. 'Bye."

He left the chemist's shop and headed back home to collect his kit for the pool and gym with mixed thoughts as he walked towards the flat. After his talks with Dr Bowden and the pharmacist he hoped there would be no more daft dreams about a twin sister or disfigured people from the past. It seemed it was a blunder by the chemist that had led to the mix-up over his tablets but the pharmacist's description of the woman was almost identical to Jenny Potter's. On the other hand, if the blood sample showed traces of illegal substances he would have some tricky questions to answer.

Checking his mailbox in the entrance hall of his flat he found just one letter and a note that had been pushed under the door. The note was from Ernie, it read: "Vic. Sorry I can't make this afternoon for your session, I'm taking Natalie to see someone at about 2.30. See you at 3.30 pm instead and don't be late this time. Ernie."

Damn, thought Vic, I really want to get on with this training, maybe I can go in for a short extra session on my own, he mused. He climbed the stairs to the flat and entered. After his recent dreams he had got into the habit of checking everything was in order. No more sunny tablets, no more ghostly visitors, he thought with a smile.

He made himself a coffee while deciding what to do next. While waiting for the kettle to boil he opened the single item of mail collected from the mailbox. It was a little bulky and Vic glanced at the postmark which he could just about make out as being from Southend. He couldn't think of anyone he knew in that town. The first line of the address sent a shiver down his back. It read 'Maudlin Nursing Home for the Elderly.'

The kettle boiled and he made the coffee with a slightly shaky hand. He placed the cup on the kitchen table and sat down. Apart from the letter there was another sealed envelope in the package. The letter was from the matron of the home and it read:

"Dear Mr Holland,

I am writing to inform you that your second cousin, Doris Denman, sadly passed away just under four weeks ago on 20 September after a long illness. I was hoping to make contact with you before the funeral but I was not able to do so and Ms Denman was cremated on 29 September with no one but myself in attendance.

She had very few personal effects and she requested that these be sold and any money received should be passed on to a local charity. This wish has been met.

However, she left instructions that the enclosed envelope should be passed on to you upon her death. It has taken me a great deal of trouble to obtain your contact details.

If there is anything else I can be of assistance to you with, please do not hesitate to contact me at the above address.

Yours sincerely,
Miss D Popperwell, (Matron)

Vic turned his attention to the sealed letter. An increasing feeling of trepidation came over him as he carefully opened it. Inside were two items, the first was another letter in his mother's unmistakable elegant handwriting. Even before starting to read its contents Vic felt his emotions begin to rise up inside. The letter began:

"My dear Victor,

As I write this letter I feel a sense of shame that I did not tell you these facts when we were together. I have no defence for this except to say that as the years went by it became harder and harder for me to build up the courage to tell you.

I have always called you my only child and I loved and treated you as such. But my wonderful son there is something you have a right to know.

You were my first born but not my only child. When I gave birth to you, I and the doctors didn't realise at the time, I was expecting twins. About five minutes after you were born I felt further movements inside me and the midwife told me there was another baby on the way. I was surprised and overjoyed at the prospect of twins, they would have been the first in our family history.

However this feeling of elation soon turned to worry when the doctor quickly took the second baby out of the delivery room. The midwife tried to reassure me and passed you to me to hold. You were so beautiful and I soon got the hang of feeding you. But nobody would tell me anything about the other baby, all the staff would say was that she was being cared for by others. At least I knew I also had a daughter.

Your father couldn't visit me for a couple of days because he was prevented from returning to Britain by bad weather, but as soon as he came to my bed I knew there was something wrong.

I had just finished feeding you when he arrived and I passed you to him to hold. He did so with great pride but there was still that feeling of something not right about his manner. Your father could never keep a secret from me and when I asked him what was wrong he burst into tears and sat there holding you. At first I thought something was not right with you, your sister was being looked after by the other staff or so I thought.

A nurse came over and took you from him and put

you in the cot. Your father came and sat on the bed and simply said, 'She's gone.'

I knew immediately who he meant, don't ask me how, I just knew he was talking about your sister. I got out of bed, walked past you in the cot and your father sitting on the bed and walked as fast as I could towards the special unit, calling out "Janet, Janet," the name I had chosen for my daughter.

One nurse took charge of you and another brought your father along to the door where I was standing calling out your sister's name. We were led into a side room and the Ward Sister came in and explained what had happened. Janet was much smaller than you and she suffered from severe breathing difficulties. There was nothing they could do for her and she died less than forty-eight hours after her birth. I asked if we could see her. They brought her little body in and we both held her.

She was as beautiful as you, Victor, with the same little mark on the side of her nose, just like you. I feel ashamed to say this, Victor, but I couldn't pick you up to feed you for nearly a week. You had to be bottle fed during that time. Please understand, it wasn't that I didn't want you it was simply that after I held Janet in my arms I simply couldn't face holding another baby. I have never forgiven the hospital staff for not letting me hold Janet while she was still alive, we didn't even have the opportunity to register her birth until your father threatened them with legal action. But once I had picked you up, Victor, I didn't want to be parted from you for more than was absolutely necessary. I felt a tinge of jealousy each time someone else held you, even your father.

Anyway, despite these failings of mine, you have grown up to be a son any mother would be proud of bringing into this world.

I will understand if you cannot forgive me for not telling you these details when we were together, I have no excuse except for a lack of courage on my behalf. I should have told you when your father was alive but after he died I couldn't bear to give you any more pain. By the time you read this letter I will have been reunited with Janet and your father and we shall watch over you with great love. If you have no one to hold, hug the bedclothes my dear.

Your ever loving mother"

Vic didn't know how long he sat by the table holding the letter but when he finally reached for his cup of coffee it was quite cold. He put the letter down and unfolded the other single sheet of paper that had accompanied his mother's letter. Even though he felt he was prepared for this official confirmation that he was one of twins

Vic could no longer hold back the tears. His body rocked with each sob of anguish. He had not cried like this, even when his mother had died.

He fell forward onto the table, knocking the cup and its contents onto the floor, along with the letter from the matron. His heavy sobs rocked the table and he was oblivious to the sound of the telephone.

He must have fallen asleep in that position and only awoke to the ringing of the phone once again. He ignored its irritating ring and it soon cut into the answer phone. Ernie's voice sounded very annoyed as he left his message. "Vic, where the hell are you, this is the third time I've rung in the last hour. Get back to me pretty damn quick or I've got a mind to call the whole deal off. It's four-fifteen now, so if I haven't heard from you by five o'clock, just forget it pal!" And the receiver was slammed down.

Stuff you Newsham, Vic said to himself, I couldn't care a

monkey's about our deal. He looked at the mess on the kitchen floor. The broken coffee cup, a damp patch on the carpet with the letter, now stained, lying under his chair. Sod that as well, nobody else is going to see it, that can wait until later, or never, depends on how I feel.

He went to the toilet and after putting the bathroom light on looked in the mirror and noticed that one of his shirt sleeves was damp. He took off the shirt and threw it on the bathroom floor and returned to his favourite living-room chair. Slumped in the chair, his thoughts were drawn back to his mother's letter. What else hadn't she told him? What other family secrets had been kept from him? There had been plenty of time to explain after his father had died so what was the big deal in not telling the truth?

The more Vic thought about his past family life the more confused he became and he felt the trickle of tears down his cheeks. Wiping them away did no good, they flowed all the more. They eventually stopped and he dozed off again. The sound of another bell awoke him from his slumbers; this time it was the doorbell and it wouldn't stop ringing. Why can't they leave me in peace, if I stay up here they'll get fed up and go away.

But Natalie didn't give up that easily. She could see the light shining in the bathroom and was convinced Vic was in his flat. She had been with Jenny Potter for most of the day and there were some questions that bothered her and only Vic could answer them.

The rain came down even heavier but that didn't bother Natalie, she was accustomed to much more severe weather conditions where she came from. As well as ringing the bell she started banging the door with her fist. Unnoticed by Natalie the middle-aged woman approached the door of the building with a key in one hand, an airline bag over one shoulder and dragging a heavy suitcase with the other. She tapped Natalie on the shoulder.

"Excuse me, dear, are you looking for someone?"

Natalie turned around to see a rather tall, gaunt-looking woman standing beside her. "Oh, yeah, I've been trying to rouse Vic. I know he's in, there's a light on up there."

"Perhaps he left it on before going on duty, Mr Holland is a policeman you know."

"I know he's a policeman but he's been off sick for the past couple of weeks and I was worried about him," Natalie replied, hoping that her show of concern might sway the woman into letting her in.

"Oh dear, has he? I've been away for the past few weeks, visiting my sister and her family in Canada. I do hope Mr Holland is all right. Let me open the door and we can go and have a look."

She placed herself between Natalie and the door and put the key in the lock. Pushing open the door, she stepped inside and turned to Natalie. "You wait here in the hallway out of the rain. I'll only be a few minutes while I put my case in and check the rest of the flat. Promise you won't wander off?" she said.

Before entering her flat the woman switched on a dim light in the hallway that barely illuminated the bottom few steps of the stairway. Natalie nodded. As long as you're no more than thirty seconds, she vowed to herself. More than a minute passed and Natalie could hear the woman opening and closing doors in her apartment. Unable to wait any longer she mounted the stairs as quietly as she could.

There was only one door at the top of the stairs and another faint light was visible inside. This had to be Vic's apartment, Natalie surmised. There was a doorbell on the frame of the door which she pressed, suddenly realising she didn't know what she was going to say when Vic answered the door.

"Hello? Are you still here?" came the woman's voice from the hallway below, followed by the sound of her footsteps as she climbed the stairs. She arrived at Natalie's side just as Vic opened the door.

Both women were taken aback by his slightly dishevelled state. Vic's eyes were slightly puffy, he had coffee stains on the front of his t-shirt and down the front of his trousers. The woman was first to speak. "Are you alright, Mr Holland? Your girlfriend didn't have a key and she was worried about you so I let her in."

Seeing Vic's bemused look, Natalie took the initiative, stepped forward and planted a kiss on his cheek before turning to the woman. "Sorry, I didn't get your name but thanks for your help," Natalie said over her shoulder as she took Vic's arm and neatly turned him around so that he was facing into his flat once more.

"Oh, I'm Gemma Watson and it was my pleasure. If there is anything else…" but the door was closed before she could finish.

So she smiled to herself, turned around and went back down the stairs to her own apartment. Now was not the time to have detailed conversations with the couple, they needed time to get to know each other before they faced a very testing time together.

9

"So now you've decided that I need a girlfriend and that you fit the bill," Vic said over his shoulder as he led the way into the living-room, "and who was your companion outside?"

"She had a key to the front entrance and let me in, lives downstairs I believe. Looks like she was just returning from a trip abroad as she had a large suitcase and an airline bag. Haven't you met her before?"

"No, never seen or heard anyone else in the building," Vic replied without turning around.

Natalie couldn't help noticing the mess on the kitchen floor as she followed him. "Well, you sure as hell need someone to bring some order into your life, judging by the mess in the kitchen and on your clothes," she retorted.

"Just a mishap with a cup of coffee, that's all. No big deal. But what do I owe this unexpected visit to, you haven't taken on work as a mobile cleaner have you?" was Vic's slightly sarcastic reply.

Natalie bit her bottom lip. She needed some information from Vic and getting involved in a petty argument with him wouldn't help her in her quest. "Sorry, it's none of my business how you live your life. Look, I can make us both some coffee if you want to change into something else. I need to talk to you and ask some questions if you don't mind," she said in a softer, disarming voice.

"Talk? What do we have to talk about? I thought that after this morning's meeting I would be the last person you would want to converse with."

"OK, maybe I was a bit touchy this morning but I've spent the best part of the afternoon with Jenny Potter, and well, there were some things that came up and you might be able to throw some light on, let's say areas of interest to me. Anyway, time for coffee?" and she gave him a smile that had won over others in the past. Vic was no different.

"It better be worth it. Coffee and sugar are in the cupboard next to the cooker, no milk for me. I'll jump in the shower so give me a few minutes before you make it."

After the devastating news he had read earlier, Vic felt slightly relieved that he could concentrate on something else for a while, like Natalie. Here's hoping he could make a better impression on her than he had done that morning. He grabbed his bathrobe from the bedroom and headed for the shower.

Natalie went into the kitchen and started to clear up the mess on the table and floor, picking up the two letters thinking they were just bills of some kind. It was only on starting to wipe the dampness off the papers and checking if any of the print was smudged that she paid closer attention to their contents. Once she had started to read the first letter from the matron Natalie found it impossible to put them down until she had read each letter twice. She was now feeling a slight pang of guilt at having read someone else's private mail. Poor guy, what a way to find out, she thought.

Quickly clearing up the rest of the mess Natalie now had a dilemma. How could she bring up the reason for her visit after reading Vic's bad news. But he might have the answers to her own problem. Well girl, let's see how much you really picked up when you majored in psychology, she thought. Placing the letters on the radiator to dry she concentrated on making the coffee. Rather than wait for Vic in the kitchen where he would notice the papers Natalie took the coffee into the living area. Placing the two cups on the low corner table she went to sit in the comfy-looking armchair.

Yet another piece of paper lay on the floor beside the chair and she reached down to pick it up.

"Thanks, I'll take that!" Vic said in a calm but firm voice.

Natalie gasped, she had not even heard him enter the room. "Do you always creep up on girls like that?"

Vic said nothing as he took the paper from her hand and went into the kitchen. Moments later he returned with the other two papers and put them on the arm of the settee and sat down. After what seemed an age to Natalie he spoke. "So now you know my family's secret as well."

Natalie felt herself blush as she tried to offer an apology. "Look, I'm sorry, I was only …"

Vic held up a restraining hand, "I know, you were only trying to help. Let's leave my life to one side and tell me, what brings you here on such a miserable night, especially after our first encounter this morning?"

It was Natalie's turn to get up without answering as she picked up one cup and offered it to Vic. She went back to sit down in the same chair and noticed how cold she felt, where moments before, it had been comfortably warm. She was about to get up and stand by the gas fire which was on a low heat, but just as quickly she felt the warmth once again. Vic noticed her restless movements and asked, "Got the fidgets?"

"I'm sorry? I've not heard that expression before?" asked Natalie.

"Never mind, it just means you don't seem comfortable where you're sitting. Sit here next to me if you want, don't worry I've just had a shower," Vic offered.

"Uh, no thanks. I just felt a little shiver but it's OK now."

Natalie stayed silent for a few moments, unsure if she could bring up the reason for her visit, especially after reading Vic's mail. Sensing her unease he said quietly, "Have you ever received such unexpected news like that?"

Natalie blushed slightly and opened her mouth to protest her innocence but Vic held up his free hand, smiling slightly as he spoke. "It's a quite natural thing to do when you pick up a damp piece of paper. You check to see if the print on it has smudged. And in doing so, you're eyes are drawn to a few words and its difficult to stop reading at least a couple of sentences. Am I right?"

Natalie's face coloured a little more as she busied herself by drinking her coffee. Putting her cup down on the table, she was about to apologise when an icy blast seemed to surround her, forcing a gasp from her lips and where moments before she had a warm glow to her cheeks, they were now almost ashen. Aware that something was not right, Vic sat forward on the settee and asked, "Everything OK? You look as if you've seen …"

The last words trailed as he realised what he was about to say. No, No, this wasn't happening, I've stopped taking those bloody tablets which caused those hallucinations.

It was Natalie's turn to see a sudden change in her companion's demeanour. She stared at him but Vic could not meet her gaze, he stood up and moved towards the bookcase and pretended to busy himself with a search of the shelves. Natalie was not fooled, there was more than just the letters that were bothering her host.

"I spent a few hours with Jenny Potter this afternoon and she told me about your accident in my grandfather's old shop. Are you up to talking about it or shall I come back another time?" she asked quietly.

Vic busied himself for a few moments longer but when he turned around he had regained his composure. "Only up to a point, as it could be subject to a criminal investigation. What is it you want to know?"

"You showed Jenny a cigarette lighter that belonged to my grandfather, can I see it please?"

"Sorry, no I can't let you have a look, the police have got it for checking for fingerprints etc. But when they've finished with it I'm sure you can get it back as you're his next of kin."

"That would be nice, I don't have anything to remember him by, But Jenny mentioned a couple of other things as well, OK if I carry on?"

Vic nodded.

"You asked her if my grandfather had a limp, why?"

Vic sat back down on the settee, looked up to the ceiling and then down at his hands. I'll have to tell someone sooner or later, he thought it might as well be Natalie since she is connected in a roundabout way. He took a deep breath, hoping he didn't get the same reaction from Natalie as earlier in the day. "I told you I'd seen a photograph of you with Mr Stockwell standing behind you this morning. Until Jenny described him to me I had no idea who he was. You might find the next bit a little difficult to take in."

He finished the rest of his coffee before continuing. "Oh, by the way, did Jenny tell you the reason I was in your grandfather's old shop?"

Natalie nodded.

"OK, this is everything I can remember about being rescued. Once the two thugs ran away after trapping me under the floorboards with the small fire I managed to push the embers away with a combination of my hands and feet. That's how I got burnt, although there isn't much to see now."

He briefly showed his hands to his guest before continuing. Natalie looked a little puzzled at the lack of any damaged tissue.

"Yes, I know what you're thinking, no signs of burn marks. I'll explain in a minute. Anyway, back in the building, I managed to partially get out of the hole in the floor but didn't have the strength to fully climb out. I was also choking on the smoke.

"The next thing I remember was a tall thin man half lifting and supporting me to get out of the hole. He led me over to the wall near the doorway and sat me down in the cold air. He disappeared for a few moments and came back with some cream of some kind that he spread gently over my hands which had blistered quite badly. It was the pain from those burns that kept me from passing out. The man said something and as I heard sirens in the distance he just disappeared. He walked with a limp and was the same man I dreamt about in the photograph with you."

Natalie said nothing for a few moments and as she stood up from the chair she asked in a slightly husky voice, "I'd like to use the bathroom if that's OK. And another drink of something a bit stronger than coffee?"

She didn't wait for Vic's permission before walking out of the room. He sat still, wondering if he had been wise to tell her everything. I think we both need something stronger, he agreed.

To his dismay, all he found in his drinks cupboard were two bottles of real ale and a bottle of red wine he was hoping to keep back in the hope of entertaining a female companion. This wasn't exactly a celebration but the label on the wine bottle brought a wry smile onto his features. It came from South America, produced by Castell Diablo, roughly translated it meant the cellars of the devil. He found a couple of wine glasses, washed and dried them and uncorked the bottle. Natalie came back into the room, looking fresh and calm.

"Sorry, there isn't much choice, either the wine or one bottle of beer each. I think I need more than one drink. Is that OK?"

She nodded and sat down while Vic poured the wine. He passed her a full glass and went and sat down on the settee. Neither spoke for a couple of minutes, both deep in thought while taking sips of wine.

Vic decided it was time to carry on his story. "I was taken to hospital and kept in for observation mainly and the coughing fits I was experiencing due to smoke inhalation. There was a small smear of the cream on the sleeve of my uniform and the doctor who was treating me had tried to get it analysed but without success."

He took a couple of sips of his wine and when Natalie said nothing he continued, "Jenny told me of the time when she was small and how she had scalded herself and your grandfather had put some cream on her burns and they disappeared by the next morning. She also told me how your grandfather also treated a young lad who had badly burnt his hand only a few days before he died in the fire. I'm just one of many who are grateful to him, he must have been quite a remarkable man, as Ernie Newsham told me about some of his other qualities."

"He was planning a surprise visit to be with me when I graduated and really would have been in the photograph with me. That's what makes your story so spooky," Natalie said quietly, still with a trace of emotion in her voice.

It was Vic's turn to feel uncomfortable. Only earlier today, he thought he had discovered the reason for his hallucinations after his visit to the doctor. But now, the letters from his mother and Natalie's comments forced him to once again contemplate what he had hoped to dismiss as sheer fantasy.

"Tell me how you got hold of the lighter?" Natalie asked. Vic didn't answer and she asked him if that was one of the things he couldn't discuss. Still no response from her host. She moved over to his side on the settee and he suddenly came out of his trance.

"Sorry, did you say something?" he asked. Natalie repeated her question about the lighter and added, "Look Vic, if you don't want to talk about this right now, I'll come back another time when you've got over the shock of your news."

"No, no it's not just that." He paused, took a deep breath and continued, "I'll tell you about the lighter but there are some other things that don't make sense to me and I can't think of a way to explain them to you because they sound so bloody illogical, excuse my French, and being a policeman I'm only supposed to deal in factual evidence. But if I told the facts as only I know them, I'd probably get locked away in the funny farm!"

A faint smile passed over her lips and she spoke softly. "You'll have to talk about it sooner or later, why not use me as your sounding board?"

Vic looked at her and smiled back. "Do you want me to lie on the settee so you can wave your watch or whatever you use to put your patients into a trance?"

Natalie got up to sit back in the chair but as soon as she sat down another icy blast seemed to engulf her and she almost leapt out of the chair and moved back to the settee to join Vic. "Is there a window open somewhere, Vic? I keep feeling cold at odd moments."

That was music to Vic's ears, at least he hadn't imagined that same sensation and his voice was more relaxed as he spoke. "Natalie, that cold feeling you keep getting is just part of the story so if you're prepared to listen to a madman's ramblings I'll tell you everything.". She nodded and took a sip of her wine.

Vic didn't leave any details out, he even included his theory on someone breaking into the Stockwell flat and possibly suffocating the old man in his sleep. Natalie paled slightly as he mentioned this but stayed silent. The dreams, his supposed visit by his dead sister, the unexplained arrival of the lighter and his visit to the doctor who implied Vic might be taking illegal substances.

Natalie waited until he had finished his story, stood up and topped up both of their glasses with more wine before excusing herself to go to the bathroom once again. She returned and sat by Vic's side, gently taking hold of his right hand in hers and examining it carefully. "Come to think of it, I do remember my mother telling my step-father about Jenny Potter's accident and how the cream seemed to work a miracle. And after seeing your hands I can't think of any other way to describe its effect."

She went back to the chair, sat back and took a large sip of wine. "Before my mum and I emigrated to Canada I used to see other children, or at least I thought I saw them in my room. But they weren't dressed in clothes I'd seen before, they wore what looked like striped pyjamas and their heads were shaved.

"When I told my mum about these visitors she said not to worry about them but on no account must I tell grandma. She was always nervous about talking on anything linked with spiritual matters when her mum was around. She told me that she had similar dreams and had mentioned them to friends at school and they had laughed and made fun of her. All except Jenny Potter. She didn't tell her mother what her so-called friends had called them both and thought that if I mentioned my dreams it would upset grandma"

"So did you mention these dreams to anyone else?" Vic enquired.

"It came up in a group discussion with other psychology students when we were having drinks at an ex-boyfriend's flat. I emphasise the word 'ex' as the bastard poked so much fun at me I swear he was out to humiliate me! I haven't mentioned those episodes since."

Vic made a mental note of how Natalie had changed from mentioning her 'visitors' to her room when she was young to just being dreams. Without realising what he was saying Vic blurted out, "I thought I was dreaming when I saw the apparition of my sister but my doubts are increasing about what did happen. And since you mentioned seeing children in striped pyjamas, didn't anyone ever tell you of your grandmother's past?"

"I know she was a refugee from Europe, why, do you know any more?"

Only what Jenny Potter told me. Your grandmother was sent to this country from Germany in early 1939, her family were part Jewish."

He didn't have to say any more, the full realisation of Vic's statement came home to Natalie and she covered her face with both hands. She stayed in this position for a couple of minutes and only sat back in her chair when Vic topped up her wine glass with the remaining contents of the bottle.

Vic leaned slightly forward as he spoke. "Ernie might know a bit about your family's background, he talked a lot about the help he was given by your grandparents. Do you want to find out more or leave things in the past, where they belong?"

She hesitated before replying. "I probably will ask him if he knows anything, but I certainly don't want to find out my family history in the same way you did…" Her voice trailed off as she realised she might have offended her host.

To her surprise Vic sat back and gave a little laugh. "If I had a choice of finding out about my family history, it certainly wouldn't have been this way. I'd have gone to a medium or clairvoyant or whatever they're called. Not that I ever believed in such daft ideas. Well, not before all this mess, now, I don't know what to think."

Natalie said nothing so Vic tried to change the subject. "How long are you staying for? I mean, have you any plans to explore other parts of the country?"

Natalie gave a little sigh. "I was planning on visiting a few sights in London and maybe a short trip to Scotland before flying back. I'm in no great rush as my ticket is open-ended for up to three months."

Natalie looked at Vic who was sitting quite upright and staring back at her. "Is something wrong, Vic?" she asked, unsure as to why her last comment was so interesting to him.

Vic's mind was suddenly whirring with all kind of thoughts;

he took a couple of moments to answer. "Look, you may not know the answers to my next question but let's give it a try. Did your grandfather have an open-ended ticket like you?"

"Yes, he did. He had a ticket that was valid to travel to Canada and back any time within a three month period."

"Is that normal? I mean, don't you have to have at least a set start date for your journey?"

"That's the normal way but in exceptional circumstances, like if you have health issues that stop you travelling at short notice, some airlines will allow some flexibility as long as you give something like twenty-four hours' notice, and as long as there is a seat available. What's so special about that Vic?"

He sat forward in his chair. "This is quite a long shot but I don't know if it's been checked out, so let me know what you think." He took a quick drink from his glass and shared his thoughts with her. "If someone did break into your grandfather's flat, found the ticket and then sold it on at a cut price to someone else, could that person have used that ticket to fly to Canada in your grandfather's place?"

"It depends on whether the travel agent who sold the ticket in the first place made a note of my grandfather's passport details. Some agents in Canada insist on seeing passports when you buy an international ticket. What's it like over here?" she replied, warming to Vic's line of thought.

"Don't know," he replied after a few moments thought, "but someone who will know is Ernie, he flew to Australia the day before the fire. It's not too late, I'll give him a ring now."

Vic left the room to use the phone in his bedroom; there were a couple of questions he wanted to ask Ernie that he didn't want Natalie to hear at this time. He was prepared for an ear-bashing from Ernie after his failure to turn up for his training session that afternoon but it would be a small price to pay if he was given the information he required. However, there was no hint of malice or lecturing; Ernie couldn't have been more helpful and this slightly puzzled Vic.

***

After the conversation ended, Ernie put down his phone and turned to his two visitors. "As I was saying, the police now have that lighter with your prints on it and Holland picked up on your accent, Mark. Everyone round here thinks you're just a baby-faced kid, not a twenty-four-year-old but you act like a kid by hanging onto a bloody lighter that can incriminate us all!"

Mark glared back at Ernie, he hated that term, baby-faced, but said nothing. Ernie continued. "Right, there's a couple of jobs I need you two to carry out, one tonight and another in the morning. Let's concentrate on tonight first. Take the van and load as much stuff as you can for the market man and deliver it to him so he can flog it at his stalls tomorrow. I'll ring him after you leave and agree a price, no big items like TVs or computers, he needs more notice to get rid of those. Finally, I want you back here tomorrow morning by eleven to sort out that other little item."

"What about that nosey copper?" Gerry, the younger of the two men spoke. Ernie laughed. "I'm sure he won't resist the opportunity to take the bait. Come into my parlour said the spider to the fly," and the others joined in, laughing.

***

Vic returned from his phone call after ten minutes, during which time Natalie went into the kitchen to make them both another cup of coffee. Vic came back into the room, looking and feeling very pleased with himself, something that had not happened in a long while. He pointed at the cup of coffee on the table and asked if there was any sugar in the cup. Natalie replied by holding up one finger.

"OK," he said in a triumphant voice, "Ernie took your grandfather to the travel agent to collect his ticket but they didn't check his passport because he didn't have one!"

"I don't understand, of course he must have had one or how else could he have travelled?" Natalie asked, slightly irritated at Vic's seemingly obvious mistake.

"Very true, but what I meant was he didn't have his passport with him because the old one had expired and the new one had been delayed in the post. Your grandfather, according to Ernie, had checked with the passport office about the delay and it was being sent by courier to arrive the next morning. By then of course, the fire had taken place and nothing could be delivered to his address. I can only assume the courier returned it to the passport office."

Natalie tried to speak but Vic held up his hand for silence. "Hang on, there's more. Normally the travel agent wouldn't have handed over the ticket but as he knew your grandfather from help he had over a health issue, he broke the rules on the understanding that Robin would bring in the passport the next morning so that the details could be verified. Of course that never happened and the travel agent kept quiet in case he got into trouble and lost his licence to operate."

"Did Ernie mention anything about grandpa buying any foreign currency?" she enquired. Vic smiled. "So, I'm with an aspiring detective. Yes, your grandpa changed £1500 into Canadian dollars. That's why Ernie insisted on taking him to get his ticket and the money, he didn't want anyone to mug the old chap on his way home."

"So there would be no way of telling if the money and ticket were destroyed in the fire," Natalie concluded. Vic smiled again. "But there is one long shot I want to try. Ernie told me which travel agent they visited and in the morning I'm going to call on them to check if it's possible after all this time to find out if that ticket was ever used. If it was, then the police have to take another look at the case."

"What time will you go there? Ernie is going to show me around the youth centre he runs in the morning, could we make it after then?"

"Sorry, Natalie, I have an appointment at the doctor's late morning and this can't wait as far as I'm concerned. Maybe we can have lunch after?" Vic hoped she would agree.

"OK," she replied rather reluctantly, then looking at her watch, "God, is that the time, I'll have to go soon."

"There's a spare bed here if you want," Vic said as innocently as he could.

"Vic, we've only just started to talk on friendly terms, I need to know a man a whole lot more before I stay over for the night. Besides, I don't know what plans your ghostly friend might have in store for us," smiling disarmingly as she finished speaking, "so can you ring for a taxi please."

"OK, if you want to leave me to the mercies of the unknown, be it on your head," Vic replied with a feeling of resignation.

"Oh come on Vic, you're a policeman, if any ghost turns nasty just show them your truncheon!" And as Vic let out a laugh, Natalie blushed to near scarlet. She turned away from him to hide her embarrassment at the double meaning of her words and then motioned for Vic to use the phone. While waiting for the taxi Vic found out that Natalie was living in her own place in Vancouver. Her stepfather, Frank Jardine, was still in Toronto but they always tried to meet up at least once every couple of months. There was nobody else she had an attachment to anywhere in the world, which was music to Vic's ears.

Ten minutes later as he came back into the entrance hall of the building the lady from the flat below was standing in the doorway and said, "Your lady friend has left, and who was the old gentleman who watched her get into the taxi? He looked very similar to her. An uncle or maybe grandparent perhaps? By the way, Mr Holland, I'm Gemma Watson, do you have a few minutes to have a little introductory chat? I can put the kettle on if you would like a cup of tea."

Vic replied, "No, I never saw anyone, Ms Watson, and I'm sorry but it's rather late and I have a lot to do tomorrow. Perhaps we can talk some other time. Goodnight." And he went back upstairs to his flat.

Once again Gemma smiled and spoke quietly, "Yes Victor, tomorrow is going to be a very busy day for you and others near to you."

10

Maybe it was the effects of the alcohol; the long evening in good company, but Vic had a decent night's sleep and awoke the next morning, ready to test his theory of the night before.

After a shower and a large breakfast that made a mockery of his fitness regime Vic dressed, having decided to delay his visit to Dr Bowden until he had called on someone else as his first priority. First, he was going to visit the travel agent to check on his theory.

There were two travel establishments in town but Ernie had not specified which one he had taken Robin Stockwell to so Vic chose the one that had been open the longest. The other business was quite new and had only been trading for about nine months. Andrew Phillips Travel Service was at the end of a rank of three shops in a single storey building. The middle premises next door to the travel agent's were boarded up.

A young couple were the only other customers in the travel agent's when Vic arrived. The female assistant asked Vic if she could help and he enquired if there were any brochures on Canada. The assistant directed him to the top row of the display near the window. Vic thanked her and busied himself looking at what was on offer, hoping the couple would either leave or ask the assistant for some help.

The latter happened and the assistant invited the couple to sit at her desk. When he was sure that they were in the process of making a booking, Vic wandered over and asked in a very polite voice, "I do apologise for interrupting but is there anyone else who can help me, I am in rather a hurry."

The assistant hesitated, she didn't want to lose the booking she was processing, but a second potential customer for the business was too good to miss. She picked up the phone and spoke to someone. "The manager will be here to assist you in a moment, Sir, if you would like to take a seat by the other desk."

Vic nodded in gratitude, apologised for his interruption and moved over to the other desk. Almost before Vic made himself comfortable in his seat a middle-aged man came out of a back office and sat down opposite him. "Interested in a trip to Canada are we, Sir? Is that for business or pleasure then?"

Vic could sense the man mentally adding up his profit on such a trip and took an instant dislike to the manager. He had planned on bringing up the reason for his visit in a more discreet manner but on meeting the man he decided to take the direct route. "Neither I'm afraid, I need some information on a possible fraud that was carried out a couple of years ago," Vic said in a voice that was just loud enough to carry across the shop.

The manager's face went quite ashen as he looked over Vic's shoulder to his assistant, who had obviously heard Vic's comment and was busily trying to distract her customers from taking an interest in what was happening elsewhere. The manager regained his composure and invited Vic to follow him into his office. After closing the door behind Vic he became more confident and said, "I don't know who you are but you'd better explain yourself or I'll have a mind to call the police. You can't just walk in off the streets and accuse me of fraud."

"Mr Phillips, you are Andrew Phillips?" Vic asked and the man nodded. "You could call the police, Mr Phillips, but I think you should hear what the fraud concerns before you make that decision. I'm a police officer, though my visit to you today is not official business. But depending on your answers that might well change."

Phillips hesitated; there were a number of things from his past business dealings that might prove awkward if the authorities started to take a close interest. But which one was this stranger alluding to at this moment? He motioned to Vic to continue.

Vic began. "You may remember an incident that took place a couple of years ago that led to the death of Robin Stockwell, the retired pharmacist. I understand that Mr Stockwell collected his airline tickets for his trip to Canada the day before he died."

Phillips began to realise that this man knew details that could have only come from one source. Ernie Newsham. "If, as you claim, you are a police officer, I would like to see some form of identification before this conversation goes any further," Phillips said, trying to sound full of confidence, but Vic was not fooled by his bravado. He quietly produced his warrant card and his host slumped back in his chair and said, "I've been waiting for someone to call ever since I told Ernie that the ticket purchased by poor Robin had been used."

It was Vic's turn to show surprise. "When did you tell Ernie this? And what did he say?"

"I told him as soon as he got back from his Australia trip, he told me not to mention it to anyone until he had dealt with things and given me the all clear. Needless to say, I haven't heard anything on this matter from him since."

Vic sat back and stared up at the ceiling. Why would Ernie want such information kept quiet? Surely he would know this kind of evidence could have made all the difference between an accidental death inquest and a possible murder enquiry. "OK, let me deal with the Ernie issue. Did you keep the details of who used the ticket? Maybe I can follow things up from that direction."

Phillips gave a little smile as he replied, "I don't think that will help you much. You see, the man who used the ticket naturally used a false name." Phillips held up a hand as Vic tried to interrupt. "You were going to say the police could trace this person? Well, they did. And they discovered he was shot and killed in a shootout with the police in Canada about six months after leaving this country."

"How did you find out about that?" Vic asked.

Before Phillips could answer, there was a soft knock on the office door and the female assistant popped her head around the door. "I'm sorry for intruding, Mr Phillips, but I've finished with the customers and it's my half day and I have to go to my dentist's appointment. Do you want me to close up or will you look after the shop?"

Phillips hesitated for a moment before speaking, "Close up and put the 'Gone to Lunch' sign on the door, Karen. I'll ring you this evening to discuss things."

With a second apology she left the room and closed the office door. Phillips waited until he heard Karen leave the shop and lock the front door before looking at Vic and remembering the question his visitor had asked. "Oh yes, you wanted to know how I found out those details. Well, the man who died in Canada was from up North, Leeds I think. There was an article in a trade magazine about it several months later, including his picture, with an appeal for anyone with information about selling a ticket to that man to contact the police."

"And you didn't put two and two together I suppose," Vic said with a slight hint of sarcasm.

Phillips coloured slightly. "As a matter of fact I had my suspicions, but I could have lost my licence to trade so I asked Ernie Newsham for advice."

"Surely he told you to go to the police to at least check it out?" Vic said.

Phillips sat back in his chair and said in a quiet voice, "No, on the contrary, he said the ticket I sold to Mr Stockwell would have been destroyed in the fire and the police would not be interested. It was at this time that he told me not to tell anyone about the conversation we had about the ticket."

Vic waited quietly, he could sense that Phillips wanted to get things off his chest, perhaps hoping he could gain favour by passing on information. Phillips continued. "I keep details of all tickets and foreign currency that are handled here, and I'm sure I can provide you with those details if you think it will help your enquiries. But will I get into trouble over this? If this was to become public knowledge that I was, well, found to be covering up in some way, however indirectly, for anyone involved in Mr Stockwell's death, I would be finished in this town."

This was the breakthrough that Vic had been looking for and he responded, "If you can get me those details it will help a great deal, and who knows, might even lead to those directly involved in Robin Stockwell's death."

"But Ernie Newsham would know this, him being a former policeman? Surely he couldn't be involved in such a crime?" Phillips seemed to realise what his evidence might mean.

Vic replied, "I don't know the reason why Ernie wanted this kept quiet, but that's for others to find out. In the meantime, don't mention any of this conversation to anyone, especially Ernie. One other thing, as soon as you find out the details on the passport and Canadian money, leave a message on this number."

Vic wrote down his home telephone number and stood up. Phillips unlocked the front door of the shop to let Vic out. Before following his caller out of the door he made one final comment to him. "I won't be able to look for the details you require until tonight as I keep such sensitive information at home in a safe place. My form of insurance, you understand."

Vic nodded and smiled to himself as he went into the street. So Phillips didn't trust Ernie completely. When he obtained the papers that Phillips claimed he had, it might be time to hand it over to his superiors. But Ernie would have realised that Phillips would crack under questioning, yet he had freely given Vic these details. Why? It didn't make sense? Could there be a totally innocent explanation for Ernie withholding such information? No, he would have to be on his guard in any further dealings with friend Newsham.

Phillips locked the door behind him, explaining that he was going to buy some lunch before re-opening the shop for the afternoon. Neither of them took much notice of two figures standing by a bus shelter across the street.

As soon as Vic and Phillips had disappeared from view the two figures walked quite casually across to the travel agent's shop and finding the door locked walked quickly down an alleyway that ran alongside. One of the figures was carrying a bag that appeared quite heavy. The alley, which was wide enough for a large refuse bin to be pushed along when collections were due. turned right and continued behind the rank of shops. Opposite the rear of the shops was a ten-foot-high wall that hid all view from behind to the alley.

Mark, the older of the two, signalled silently to his companion, Gerry, to unlock the door at the rear of the travel agent's premises. Gerry reached into one of his pockets and took out a bunch of skeleton keys. Before inserting one of the keys into the lock he pressed down on the door handle, and to his surprise, the door swung open. Stepping quickly inside, the two set about their task swiftly and quietly.

Mark removed a large container filled with petrol from the bag he had carried, while Gerry disconnected the valve on the gas cylinder that was connected to a small cooker hob. He then used a couple of the tea towels that were lying on the worktop and stuffed them into the gap under the inner door. Mark took one of the mugs that was next to the small sink and filled it with petrol and placed the mug in the microwave and closed the door. He poured about half the remaining contents of the container over the work surface, finally placing the container against the inner door. Mark then opened the valve on the gas cylinder and signalled to Gerry to go outside with him.

Mark said quietly, "I'll let the fumes build up for a few minutes and then go back in and switch the microwave on. I'll give us enough time to get the hell out of here. You go back to the end of the alley to check that nobody is nosing around, but make sure you don't get spotted."

Twenty minutes after leaving, the travel agent returned to his premises. The queue in the baker's shop had been longer than he expected and he was a little annoyed at the slow service. He unlocked the door, changed the 'Gone to Lunch' sign and replaced it with one that read 'Please ring for assistance', before locking the door from the inside.

Gerry had almost missed seeing Phillips coming along the street and ran back to tell Mark. "Mark, the shop owner is coming back, we'll have to forget this lot and scarper. Ernie will have to cover his tracks some other way, I'm going to warn the guy not to go in," and he turned to run away but his stronger companion grabbed him and pulled him back.

"You're not telling anyone you gutless prat. We came here to make sure Philips doesn't spill the beans, if he's inside when this lot goes up then too bad. You panicked and smothered that old geezer a couple of years ago and I had to cover your tracks with the fire. Just Like I've been doing ever since we met. If you think I'll let you blow everything because you don't have the balls then there's only one solution left open to me and Ernie, buddy!"

Mark grabbed his colleague by the lapels of his jacket and swung him around so forcefully that the back of Gerry's head hit the brick wall with a sickening thud and his body went limp as he slid to the floor. Mark checked the back of Gerry's head and his hand was covered in grey matter. He hesitated for only a moment before dragging his former companion inside. He quickly removed the set of skeleton keys from Gerry's pocket. Then, coldly and calmly, Mark set the microwave timer to two minutes on high power and pressed the start button. With a final glance at his former partner in crime he stepped over his body, closed the outer door and walked swiftly down the alley.

Andrew Phillips went into his back office, leaving the connecting door slightly ajar and sat down to eat his lunch. The sound of raised voices coming from the alleyway was nothing unusual, so he ignored them. He made a mental note to go and check the outer door to the kitchenette as a new propane gas cylinder had been delivered that morning. Karen had let the gas delivery man in through the back door but was sometimes forgetful about locking it afterwards. He would check after finishing his lunch. Some three months earlier she had left the door unlocked and someone had helped themselves to the microwave and kettle. Fortunately the microwave had been quite an old and rather noisy model and the replacement was much quieter and did not disturb his work when in use.

As he opened the bag containing his lunch he pondered over the morning's events. Ernie knew too much about his past so he would have to be careful about what he told his morning caller. However, he didn't want to have any association with anyone who might be responsible for Stockwell's death.

He didn't notice that the microwave had been started up in the kitchenette.

He took a bite out of his sandwich but was interrupted by another sound, the doorbell ringing. He quickly swallowed what was in his mouth, stood up, and opened the office door to see who had rung the doorbell. There was no-one there so he turned around to return to his desk. As he stood in the doorway to his back office he heard the microwave running and the unmistakable smell of petrol drifted through the air.

An alarm bell rang in his head and Phillips turned to run out of the front entrance. He got to within half a dozen paces of the front door before the force of the explosion threw him across the display area of the shop and through the plate glass window that was the front of the building. He was dead before he hit the pavement. The raging fire that followed engulfed what was left of the travel agent's shop.

Moments earlier a youth had been seen ringing the doorbell and running away. About fifty yards down the road he almost knocked over an elderly lady as she came around a corner of another block of shops. Jenny Potter had made one of her rare excursions to the shopping centre.

"Get out of my bloody way you old bat," shouted Mark as he dodged past the startled woman.

Luckily, her encounter with the youth had forced Jenny to take a couple of steps backwards into the side street. She turned around to remonstrate with the youth when the explosion occurred. The corner of the nearby buildings saved the elderly lady from any injury, but as she turned to see what had happened she was confronted with the horror of the demolished travel agency and the body lying amongst the debris.

Jenny stood transfixed at the scene for what seemed like an age to her before someone stood in front of her and asked if she was hurt or needed help. Getting no response, the younger woman gently took hold of Jenny's arm and led her to a café that didn't overlook the scene of carnage. Already the sounds of emergency vehicles could be heard approaching the area.

As she sat down in the café Jenny turned to thank her helper but there was no one nearby apart from the man behind the counter. He noticed her confused look and came over to her. He was quite used to elderly folk wandering in off the street and thought this was just another resident from the sheltered housing across town. He had also heard the explosion but didn't link it with his visitor's sudden appearance. Before he could speak Jenny asked, "Where is the young lady who brought me here? I need to speak to her."

"Nobody was with you love, you came in on your own. Now what will it be, cup of tea and a muffin?"

Jenny looked around again, the café was indeed empty apart from herself and the worker. But there was a small pool of some liquid on the floor in front of her. She smiled to herself and stood up to leave. "I must find a policeman, I have something important to tell them."

Seeing he was about to lose a customer, he took Jenny's arm and sat her down again. "I'll get you a cup of tea first and then I'll call the police for you. Sit tight while I get your cake as well." He walked back towards the counter and turned round to see Jenny walk briskly out of the door.

Vic heard the same explosion as he entered the lobby area of the Youth Centre. He hesitated for a moment, unsure as to whether he should go and investigate what might have happened. After his conversation with Phillips he decided that his visit to the doctor's surgery for the blood test results could wait; speaking to Ernie was more important.

"Can I help you?" asked the female receptionist.

"Oh yes, is Ernie Newsham around please? I was supposed to meet up with him about half an hour ago but I've been held up."

"No, I'm sorry, Mr Newsham went for lunch about twenty minutes ago and said he wouldn't be back till later," she replied.

Vic turned to leave and suddenly remembered that Natalie had said she was meeting Ernie that morning. "Did a young lady come to see him this morning? She would be about five feet ten and had fair hair down to her shoulders."

The girl hesitated, so Vic produced his warrant card once again, hoping it would do the trick. It did. "Yes, that lady was here and left with Mr Newsham but she didn't look very…"

Before she could finish what she was going to say the phone on her desk rang and it was picked up in an automatic reflex.

"Excuse me. Hello, Youth Centre, Beryl speaking. Oh hi Janet. What did you say? There's been an explosion at the travel agent's? Is Karen OK?"

Vic heard the half conversation and grabbed the phone from the startled girl. "I'm a police officer. Do you know if Mr Phillips is OK?"

The news that a body was lying outside the remains of the shop sent shivers down Vic's spine. He turned to the receptionist once again. "This is important, do you know where Ernie and the lady went for lunch?"

"Well, Mr Newsham took his car keys so I assume he would have gone to the Golf Club on the other side of town. I can ring and check if you like but I need to find out if my sister Karen is OK. She works at the travel agent's shop."

"Your sister is fine, I was in the shop with Mr Phillips when I heard Karen say she was leaving early to attend her dentist's appointment. That must have been nearly an hour ago. Now will you ring the golf club and check if Mr Newsham and the lady are there."

Beryl gave a big sigh of relief, thanked Vic for the news and rang as he requested. Moments later she confirmed, "Yes, they arrived more than ten minutes ago. Do you want me to pass on any message to them?"

"No, but you were about to say something about the lady with Mr Newsham not looking very happy or something?"

Beryl blushed slightly, "Well, it was just the manner in which Mr Newsham took her arm and led her out to his car, but I could be wrong."

Vic nodded and thanked her for the call and left. It was time to pass on the information he had gathered that morning.

When Vic arrived, the police station was in the grip of a not insignificant crisis. People were dashing in and out of rooms and phones seemed to be ringing in every office. Sergeant Proudfoot saw Vic walk in and beckoned him over to the main desk.

"Holland, can you man a phone so that I can release a fit officer to carry out other tasks?"

"Of course, Sarge, but I have some information regarding the explosion that you should hear first. It's linked in with Robin Stockwell's death."

Proudfoot glared at Vic like a man about to explode. Surprisingly however, he motioned to Vic to follow him into the back office and closed the door behind them. The sergeant spoke quietly but with a hint of menace in his voice, "Holland. We are in the middle of a very serious enquiry, possibly murder, it's not clear yet. Then you walk in and try to suggest it has something to do with an accidental death some two years ago. Listen to me very carefully, if you're not off these premises in one minute I'll arrest you for wasting police time. I'll also make it my duty to have you kicked out of the force as soon as we've dealt with matters in hand. Now, get out of my sight, Holland!"

Without thinking of the consequences Vic blurted, "Sergeant, I was with Phillips no more than twenty minutes before the explosion and he was going to pass on proof about a failed bank robbery in Canada that was linked with Stockwell's death."

Proudfoot thought for a moment then spoke in a less hostile manner. "OK, go home and write out a statement of what happened between you and Mr Phillips this morning. But it better be convincing evidence or I'll carry out the second part of my promise. For your information, it's not been formally identified yet but the body is probably that of Andrew Phillips, the manager. Now don't say another word and go home to write your statement."

Vic turned and left the office and walked out of the station in a daze. No Andrew Phillips, so no proof of the link. What the hell do I do now, he thought. Suddenly he realised Natalie was with Ernie and it was important to him to make sure that she was safe before writing out his statement. The Golf Club was only a brisk ten minute walk away from the police station so he turned back from his flat and headed in the other direction.

When Natalie had arrived at the Youth Centre earlier that morning she was asked to wait in the lobby as Ernie was in a meeting with two people and could not be disturbed. She sat on the chair that was opposite the door marked Manager, rather than the more comfortable-looking settee that was placed parallel to a flight of wooden stairs.

From the outset it was clear that a heated conversation was taking place within the Manager's office. Natalie didn't want to be seen eavesdropping on a private meeting but the odd word and short phrase seeming to mention "copper" and "make sure no evidence is found," drifted her way.

She was torn between trying to listen to what else she might hear and wanting to leave and find Vic. Moments later the door opened and two youths, no she decided, one was early twenties and the other late teens, came out and walked past her.

One was carrying a bag which appeared heavy. The second younger man, walking slightly behind his companion, was smaller in build but Natalie noticed something quite distinctive about him. His left hand had been badly injured at some time in the past and had not healed properly. Her gaze followed them as they left and she didn't notice Ernie come out of the office. She also missed the frown on his face as he observed his two visitors leaving.

Ernie cleared his throat and Natalie turned quickly, her face glowing as if she had just been caught with her hand in the cookie jar. "Have you been waiting long? I had to sort out some Centre business that couldn't wait. You seem to be intrigued by Gerry's hand. No mystery really, just another kid who wouldn't listen to advice about handling fireworks. Look, I have a project you might be interested in if you intend staying around these parts for a while."

Natalie had noticed how Ernie had tried to change the

subject but she persisted in her line of probing. "I haven't decided about what my immediate plans are, I don't want to make any hasty decisions. But tell me, did his accident happen before my grandfather died? I've heard about his special burns cream, I'm sure he would have been able to help."

Ernie's features betrayed a quick flash of irritation; it disappeared just as quickly, but not before Natalie had felt a feeling of unease at the show of hostility. Ernie turned back into his office, picked up his car keys, took hold of Natalie's right arm and gently but firmly turned her around to face the lobby area. "No, he burnt his hand after your grandfather died. That's all in the past; right now I'll take you somewhere for lunch and we can discuss my proposal in more depth before you decide."

Natalie tried to stall him. "I thought you were going to show me around the Centre, and isn't Vic supposed to be joining us?"

Ernie again failed to conceal his annoyance at Natalie's questions. "Don't waste your time over that bloke Vic, I've been trying to help him get fit but he keeps failing to turn up on time. He's not worth the effort."

He briefly looked away towards the girl on reception duty. "Beryl, we're going out for an early lunch, my last meeting went on longer than expected, see you in about two hours."

He glanced at Natalie, defying her to make any further comment. She remained silent but the look of unease on her face was quite evident.

As they got out of Ernie's car in the Golf Club car park five minutes later a muffled explosion could be heard coming from the direction of the town centre. Natalie turned her head but Ernie seemed not to notice and carried on walking.

11

By the time Vic arrived at the Golf Club, Ernie and Natalie were eating their dessert. The look of relief on Natalie's face gave Vic mixed messages. Was she genuinely pleased to see him or had she been quizzed by Ernie and divulged his whereabouts of the morning.

Ernie spoke first. "Well, this is a surprise, Vic, I thought you might be coming in for another fitness session. You know, you've missed a few lately, if you keep this up it's going to be difficult to convince the medical board of your fitness."

Vic ignored his comment and went straight to the point. "Other matters had to take priority. I paid a visit to Andrew Phillips's travel shop this morning and your name came up a few times. I think you and me should pay a visit to the station to clear things up."

No hint of emotion showed on Ernie's face as he replied, "I'll be interested in what Phillips has to say but here is not the place. We'll finish our meal and after I've paid the bill we can go back to my office; there perhaps things will become a lot clearer for you.

Natalie asked Vic, "Was there something going on in town this morning? I was sure I heard some kind of explosion."

Vic nodded. "I'd just arrived at the Youth Centre when I heard it as well. Your receptionist, Ernie, got a call from one of her friends who told her that the travel agency was just a heap of rubble."

Both Natalie and Ernie looked in surprise at Vic's news but before they could ask any questions he continued, "The rest will have to wait until we get back to Ernie's place and we can compare notes."

Ernie went to the pay booth to clear his debt and was held in conversation by the club manager for a few moments. In that brief time while they were alone Natalie told Vic why she was feeling uncomfortable in Ernie's presence. "Ernie's trying to get me to assist him in running a self-defence class at the Centre tonight, and if it goes well, in his estimation anyway, he wants to make it a regular feature. I only know the bare basics of Aikido, nothing like enough to teach anyone else. Besides, the guy is beginning to give me the creeps and I've no intention of staying here long term."

Vic glanced at Ernie who had his back to them. "He told me you had a Second Dan Black Belt in Aikido when we first met, that's a lot more than just basic knowledge."

Natalie looked a little sheepish as she replied softly, "I use that line to keep the wolves at bay and you would be surprised how often it works, but I am only about to take my second grade, quite basic really."

Vic gave her a little smile. "As you said, it works so why not. I know a bit more than the basics of self-defence but I don't suppose he would want me around given what I have picked up about his little operation at the Centre. Don't worry for now, other events might give him something else to think about."

Seconds later Ernie re-joined his companions and without saying a word he motioned to them to follow him.

***

Sergeant Proudfoot looked up from his paperwork to see a familiar figure walk towards him. He let out a silent groan to himself. This was the last person he wanted to see, with all the chaos going on in town. "Ms Potter, I don't know what it is you need but we are very busy today; whatever it is, can it not wait until at least tomorrow?"

Jenny had walked to the police station after unsuccessfully trying to talk to a young constable at the scene of the explosion. She came straight to the point. "Sergeant, I was nearly knocked over by a young man as he ran away moments before the bomb blew up that shop."

Proudfoot hesitated. It was not unknown for the odd person to claim that they had information relating to a major crime. Just misguided attention seekers mostly, he would have put Jenny Potter in that group under normal circumstances. But there was something about her manner that made the sergeant decide he could spare a few minutes to hear her story. He told a WPC to take his place at the counter and motioned to Jenny to follow him into the interview room. He invited his guest to sit down opposite him. "Now, Ms Potter, I can only spare you a few minutes so please tell me what you think you saw."

Jenny told her story. "I went into town to collect a book from the library this morning and I was about to turn left out of Herbert Street when I heard the sound of someone running very fast so I slowed down before I got to the junction of Herbert and Wine Street. You see, I have been knocked over before by someone running without looking where they were going. Anyway, this youth came charging round the corner and if I hadn't slowed down he would have run straight into me and knocked me over."

"I suppose you didn't recognise him?" asked Proudfoot. Jenny hesitated. "I'm sure I have seen him somewhere before, Sergeant, but I can't remember where. But as he ran past me he turned and shouted something rather rude, like many young people of today. There was a strange smell on his clothes. I think, no I'm sure, it was the smell of bottled gas. I use bottled gas myself and that was definitely the smell."

"Is there anything else you can remember about this youth . His clothes, stature and his accent, was he local?"

Jenny thought for a moment. "I called him a youth, but he had the build of a young man. Oh, and when he shouted at me as he ran off he had a very distinct accent, North of England I would say. One more thing, Sergeant, he was wearing those trainer shoes that young people today wear instead of proper footwear and there was a silver buckle on the heel of the right shoe."

Proudfoot stood up. "Ms Potter, what you have told me is very interesting and helpful. Now I'm going to get a lady constable to come in and take a proper statement from you. She will write everything down and then ask you to check what she has written and ask you to sign the statement. I'll also get her to bring you a cup of tea. You just wait there for a few moments, she won't be long."

"Oh, I hope not, my cats will be wondering where I am, I told them I wouldn't be more than an hour and I've been out more than that now."

Proudfoot smiled. "It won't be long and when you have finished giving your statement I'll arrange for a taxi to take you home to your cats."

He was still smiling to himself when he told the WPC her task. "She may be worried about her bloody cats but I bet she will rabbit on for a good while, but make sure you get all the details from her."

Jenny sat patiently waiting for the constable to arrive, she was feeling rather important and quite liked the inner glow it gave her.

***

Both Natalie and Vic had quite different feelings to those of the elderly lady. Ernie had driven them back to the Centre in almost complete silence. Once there he had told Beryl, the receptionist, to close up and go and visit her sister who might be in a state of shock after the events of the day. There were no other clients at the Centre so he locked the main entrance and took his guests into the office.

Ernie sat down behind his desk and waited for the others to sit opposite him with their backs to the door. "OK, what did Phillips have to say for himself, bearing in mind I once had to take him in for questioning regarding a fraud investigation when I was in the force."

Rather than answer Ernie's query, Vic had decided to get straight to the point and ask about the airline tickets belonging to Robin Stockwell. "Why didn't you report that the airline ticket had been used by someone else, which would prove there had been a break-in at Stockwell's apartment?"

Natalie let out a little gasp which momentarily distracted Vic and he turned to apologise to her for not giving prior notice of what he had discovered. But even in that very brief moment, Ernie had time to open a desk drawer and take out a small handgun from within, although he also noticed something else was missing from the drawer. Natalie spotted the gun first, touched Vic on the arm and pointed across the desk.

"So that weasel Phillips gave the game away, I suppose it was only a matter of time," Ernie snarled.

"But what's your involvement in all this Ernie? Were you covering up for someone else? I thought you were my grandfather's friend," Natalie asked.

Ernie sat back and thought for a few moments, then he spoke in a cold, emotionless voice. "I was his friend, he was just an innocent victim in something far deeper but he started to ask awkward questions . And until you came onto the scene, Vic, everything was running quite smoothly. Let me explain, I was running a nice little security and protection racket around here.

"It worked like this. I visited local businesses to offer them security advice. As an ex-copper that made my role seem quite authentic. They paid a small fee for the advice and for an additional sum I would guarantee a discreet night security patrol. Some paid up, others didn't. For those who refused my offer, well certain, let's say 'accidents' would take place. Nothing too heavy at first, mind you; if they still refused to play ball then that upped the ante."

"In what way?" Vic asked.

"Anything from broken windows to damaged stock through vandalism up to 'accidental fires' in storerooms, not enough to put them out of business you understand. But if they didn't get the message, well, sometimes an example had to be made."

"Would those 'examples' be set by two kids known as Torch and Keys by any chance?"

Ernie simply nodded. Before speaking, Vic glanced at Natalie and held her hand. "So Robin Stockwell started asking awkward questions and you let Torch and Keys loose to silence him."

"I casually dropped the hint that Robin had collected his airline tickets and money from Phillips, knowing that Mark's brother was desperate to leave the country after a particular incident which involved doing me a special favour. I guessed that Mark would see it as an opportunity to help his brother go on his way. I was on my way to Australia so nothing could be pinned on me."

"You callous bastard!" Natalie shouted, and half rose from her seat but Ernie waved the gun in her direction and Vic gently but firmly pulled her back into her chair. He then looked directly at Ernie. "But why, Ernie? You had an exemplary record during your time in the force. Surely you had a good pension and other opportunities to get a decent job on the right side of the law?"

"Oh yeah, and what else did my record stand for!" Ernie replied with a heavy tone of sarcasm, "I wasn't driving that bloody patrol car when it crashed. Proudfoot was and he killed two other people in the other car. He gets made up to bloody sergeant and I get crippled out of the service. I tried staying legit but soon fell into debt so what choice did I have?"

"Surely your medical discharge from the force and your pension, along with running the Sports Centre must help. Also, I thought you said you went to Australia on a trip. That doesn't come cheap," Vic replied.

"Don't make me laugh," Ernie snarled, "I went to Australia to flog some stuff we came across in our security scam. One of our punters had a load of stolen goods that we came across. He gave it to me to get rid of, paid my fare to Australia as part of the fee for silence and I made a pretty penny out of that trip. Unfortunately he met with, let's say an accident before he could collect his share."

"Courtesy of your friends Torch and Keys again I'll bet," Vic said with equal irony.

Ernie said nothing but a smile crossed his face as a voice said, "He's quick this guy isn't he?" Mark spoke as he stood behind Vic and Natalie in the open doorway. He also had a gun in one hand. "Not quite, Mr Clever Dick. My brother, Kevin, came down that same morning Ernie flew to Australia and took care of him for us. Kevin took the punter for early morning swimming lessons in the pool next door and dumped the body in the river. Meanwhile me and Gerry picked up the ticket and money from your grandpop that same night."

Natalie let out a strangled cry and attempted to turn and rise from her chair but once again Vic held her back. Mark took a small step backwards and calmly pointed his gun at her. "Ernie told me about your self-defence capabilities, sweetie, but I bet you can't move faster than a bullet." He gave a sardonic laugh. "Your mates found the punter's body more than a year later but the coroner marked it down as accidental death. You'd be surprised how willing our other more reluctant 'clients' jumped into line once the body was found."

" Was that man's name Graham Bishop by any chance?" Vic asked casually.

"Yeah it was, friend of yours?" Mark asked. When Vic didn't reply he continued, "Anyway, now you've spilled the beans Ernie, and after me and Gerry spending half the night getting shot of some of the evidence, I'm getting a bit fed up of having to cover up other people's tracks."

"Like blowing up the travel agent's shop?" Vic said, staring straight at Mark.

"Full marks again, smart arse. If you want to know, I was only planning on warning off that worm Phillips as soon as Ernie told me he could cause trouble. I had timed it when nobody would get hurt but Phillips came back earlier than I expected from his lunch, so let's say he was in the wrong place at the wrong time. This scam was bringing in a small fortune and we had your mates chasing shadows trying to catch us. And then you stuck your big feet in where they had no business."

"What happens now?" Vic asked.

"You two are going to have to be otherwise detained while we disappear from the scene," Mark answered.

"Ernie, you know he means to kill us don't you? He's already killed at least two others and he and his mate tried to kill me before. Where is your mate by the way?"

Mark took a step forward and pointed the gun at Natalie's head. "Enough chat, copper, if you don't keep that mouth shut she gets the first bullet. And if either of you tries anything funny, the other one gets it. Now stand up slowly, step outside the office and move towards those stairs."

Vic glanced at Natalie and gave her a reassuring smile.

"Move it, lovebirds. I'm not a patient person."

The stairway was only wide enough for one person to walk

up in single file. Mark ordered Natalie to go first, followed by Vic, himself next with Ernie bringing up the rear. He gave Natalie a chilling reminder. "Remember, Girlie, any funny stuff and lover boy loses a kidney at the very least. Keep four stairs between you two and when you get to the top, turn around and walk backwards along the balcony."

Before all four started climbing the stairs, Ernie repeated Vic's question about the whereabouts of Gerry. Mark didn't reply until he reached the top of the stairs and answered without taking his eyes off Vic's back. "He's laying low for now. I'll take his share of the kitty to him after we split up."

"And what's your plans for us? Are you going to stand and watch him and do nothing, Ernie?" Vic said. He continued walking along the balcony without turning around, giving Natalie another smile as they faced each other.

"Shut up and keep walking, copper, it makes no odds to me whether I shoot you in the back or front, so no attempts at playing the hero."

Ernie remained silent as he reached the top of the stairs. Natalie spoke for the first time in several minutes. "Ernie, if it hadn't been for my grandparents helping you, you wouldn't have made a complete recovery from your accident. Is this the way you're going to repay them by allowing this maniac to kill us? You must be as sick as he is!"

"No more bloody chatter from anyone, Girlie, unlock that door you're standing by and get inside or I'll put the first bullet in lover boy. There's a light switch on the wall on your right, switch it on and stay in my view in the room. Now shift that pretty arse of yours!"

Vic motioned to Natalie with a slight nod of his head to follow the instructions.

"Good," Mark sneered, "now you copper. Get on your hands and knees and follow her in and stay in that position until I say otherwise."

Vic had little option but to obey. As he passed into the room on all fours Mark couldn't resist giving him a hefty kick to his rear which sent his victim sprawling forward, landing at Natalie's feet.

"That's enough of that, Mark." Ernie spoke for the first time since they had all climbed the stairs. Mark closed the door and locked it before facing Ernie.

Vic and Natalie strained to hear the conversation going on beyond their prison door but they couldn't get too close to the opening for fear of Mark hearing someone standing near the aperture and firing off a shot or two in their direction. Mark would be too unpredictable to take any chances when it came to a loaded gun.

Vic had found a torch in a box by his feet; along with the single light bulb in the ceiling it helped to illuminate a little extra brightness in their gloomy surroundings. Several boxes, some of which had been opened, were scattered around, other boxes were still sealed and intact.

It was like an Aladdin's cave: designer clothing, jewellery, expensive perfumes, electrical equipment including laptop computers, stereos and televisions, kitchen gadgets and even DIY and building equipment. Most of the better quality jewellery, designer clothing and accessories had been removed along with some of the smaller items of electrical equipment.

Apart from the ceiling light there was a small louvre window about three-quarters of the way up one wall in the far corner. The window was the width of a normal doorway but only about one foot high. Too small for a person to escape through.

"I hope you're not getting soft on me like Gerry did, are you, Ernie?" Mark said as he waved his gun in a menacing fashion.

Where is Gerry? You two are hardly apart, what's happened to him Mark?" Ernie demanded as he took a step towards the young thug.

"Relax, he'll be here later. Right now, we need to get as much of that stuff in the van to make one final run. We won't get as much cash as we hoped but we haven't time to haggle over prices."

"OK," Ernie agreed, "but small items only. Digital cameras, mobile phones, nothing bulky. Is your contact waiting with his helicopter? Once we get rid of this lot we'll need to get away fast."

"All arranged, he just needs forty minutes' notice and we disappear to Southern Ireland and then we can fly off from Shannon in different directions. Meanwhile your ex-mates will be thinking towards Europe if we leave some euros lying around."

Mark turned back to the locked door and rapped on it several times, calling out loudly, "If you two lovebirds know what's good for you, listen very carefully. Right, I want you standing against the wall directly opposite this door. If I don't see both of you standing against that wall I'll start shooting. And I've got plenty of ammo. Then, me and Ernie are coming in to collect some stuff, so do as you're told and maybe nobody will get hurt."

Turning to Ernie he said quietly, "You keep your gun on them while I take the stuff out."

Ernie nodded and retrieved his gun from his pocket. Unlocking the door, Mark pushed it open and checked to make sure the two prisoners were standing in the position he had indicated. Vic had switched off the torch and hid it on hearing Mark's shouts from outside the room.

"Good, now keep still while I pick up a few more goodies. Remember Ernie, any sudden moves from either, put a bullet in the nearest to you."

"Just get on with it Mark, I know what to do."

Vic said quietly, "So who is the boss, Ernie, are you going to let him turn you into a killer like him?"

"Enough chat, Vic. You just don't know when to keep your mouth shut do you! I'm sorry Natalie, if you hadn't got involved with him, you and me might have had a future together."

"Me and you? Never in a million years, you murderous bastard!"

Mark gave a short laugh and carried three boxes outside; moments later he came back in and carried two more onto the balcony. "OK, Ernie, let's go load up the van."

The two men left, locking the door behind them. After loading the goods into the van they returned to the building and Mark said, "You get the rest of the cash and our passports from the safe, I need to find something else. Meet me back upstairs."

Ernie had opened the safe and had almost completed the removal of all the money and passports when the phone rang. He let it ring several times before picking up the receiver. "Leisure Centre?" he said.

"Ah, Ernie, just the man I want to speak to. Have you seen Vic Holland lately, I need to speak to him rather urgently. He was in the travel agent's shop not long before it blew up. I take it you've heard about that?" asked his former colleague.

"Oh, Peter, it's you. No, he didn't turn up for his session this morning so I don't know where he is."

Sergeant Proudfoot frowned and said, "I was told you were talking to him at the Golf Club earlier on…"

Ernie interrupted and said in a terse voice, "I only saw him briefly, look, I've got problems with the heating here and I need to help the engineer. Speak again, 'bye," and he hung up.

Proudfoot was taken aback by his ex-colleague's manner, he had been told that Ernie and Holland had left the Golf club with a woman in Ernie's car. Leaving the office he went to the front desk and spoke to the young PC. "If the inspector wants me, tell him I've gone to the Leisure Centre to speak to Ernie Newsham. Something doesn't feel right to me."

Ernie arrived at the top of the stairs as Mark covered

something on the floor with his jacket. "Who was that on the phone just now?"

"Just one of the lads wanting to know if the Centre was open tonight for his self-defence class. I told him we were having trouble with the heating and we would be closed until further notice. What's that under your jacket?"

"Just some excess weight from the van that I don't need. There's something I forgot to pick up. There's some digital camcorders and I want to take one for myself, get one yourself for your holiday snaps if you like."

"Where's the cash and how much is there?" Mark asked as he took the key out of his pocket.

"About £30,000. That's on the office desk downstairs along with the passports. I exchanged the other £80,000 for dollars and euros last week and it's in my house' We can pick it up on the way out along with the details of the international account that was opened at the start of this venture."

Ernie stepped to one side and moved Mark's jacket with the toe of his shoe. Hidden under the jacket was a five-litre can of petrol. "No Mark, no more fires. By the time they are found we'll be long gone. I'm running the show now, so hand over your gun." And he drew out his own gun once more and pointed it at his companion.

Mark said nothing, put his jacket back on but failed to notice the dampness or the smell on the material. He turned to face Ernie and then gave a sarcastic laugh as he viewed Ernie holding the pistol. "You dumb sod!" Mark laughed again. "Make sure you've got a loaded piece before threatening me! I took the bullets out when I picked up the other gun from your drawer."

Ernie removed the magazine clip from his gun and Mark gave another cold laugh as his companion discovered the truth. Mark now pointed his own gun at Ernie and motioned to him to throw his empty weapon over the balcony. After a moment's hesitation Ernie threw the gun away and the sound of it hitting the stone floor below echoed through the building.

"If you want to know where Gerry is right now, he's under the rubble of that travel agent's shop. As I said, he got cold feet and wanted to warn Phillips so I had to stop him or we would all end up in the brown stuff. When I open the door I want you to go in and pick up the cameras."

Their raised voices had carried through the door and Vic had heard the details of Mark's betrayal and subsequent murder of his friend.

A couple of loud bangs on the door, followed by Mark's strident tones held Vic and Natalie's attention. "Listen carefully, you two. I'm opening the door so I want you both standing in exactly the same place as before. Next, Ernie is coming in to fetch something for me. Keep stock still or I might accidentally hit Ernie," he said with a sardonic laugh.

Vic switched off the torch. The door opened slowly and Ernie walked in. He avoided making any eye contact with the couple before suddenly spinning round with the intention of aiming a kick at Mark's head. However, Mark had anticipated the move and had taken a step back and not followed him into the room. As Ernie reached the apex of his attempted kick, Mark coolly fired three shots into the body of his former partner in crime who staggered back a couple of paces before crumbling to the floor.

Natalie half stifled a cry of anguish and Mark momentarily pointed the gun in her direction. "Stay exactly where you are or lover boy gets the same," Mark shouted.

Before stepping back through the door he fired one bullet at the light bulb, plunging the room into darkness. He quickly stepped backed through the doorway and locked it.

Vic retrieved and switched on the torch and dashed to see if he could help Ernie who was slumped face down over several boxes. Natalie helped to move the wounded man into a more comfortable position. He had two wounds to his chest and one to his abdomen, and let out a cry of pain as he was moved. Natalie noted the amount of blood oozing and spreading over Ernie's clothing and said quietly to Vic, "He's losing a lot of blood, we have to get him to hospital quickly or he won't make it."

Outside, Mark poured the petrol under the door, splashing some on the balcony carpet and on his clothes. He fumbled in his pockets for his spare lighter but couldn't find it. Cursing to himself he remembered it was in the van outside.

While their attention was fixed on Ernie they failed to notice liquid seeping under the door and spreading on the concrete floor towards the contents of their temporary prison. It was the odour of the liquid that alerted Vic. "Petrol! The maniac is going to set the place on fire! We've got to move Ernie to the far corner away from the door."

Ernie let out more cries of pain as they half carried him to the furthest wall away from the door.

"There must be something amongst this lot that could help us in some way to escape," Vic said, starting to rummage through the stolen goods.

Ernie pointed feebly to the far corner, "Builders' and construction gear over there."

Vic ran over to where Ernie was pointing and after a few moments he found a jack hammer, but his joy was short-lived as there was no electric plug on the end of the cable. He continued his search and eventually found two large sledge hammers and a safety harness. Vic also retrieved a packet of facial dust masks and a pair of goggles.

He crossed the room to his companions and noticed that the petrol had seeped along the floor almost to the point where Mark had earlier forced them to stand, thus dissecting the room in half. Natalie met him partway, "Ernie said there's a couple of fire extinguishers in the other corner, we might need them," and she ran past Vic before he could stop her.

He laid down the tools he had acquired and approached Ernie to check on his condition and to seek some vital information about the room. "Ernie, is there a weak point in any of the outside walls I can concentrate on to try and break out?"

Ernie opened his eyes briefly, raised one arm and pointed to the wall below the louvre window, then closed his eyes once more before Vic could ask his second question. But what was on the other side of the old doorway? What if there was a sheer drop outside? He and Natalie might be able to risk dropping down one level but there was no way they could do the same with their injured companion. As if she was reading his thoughts Natalie called out, "There's an outside balcony running round two sides of the building but there's no way to get to ground level, the stairs were removed for safety reasons."

Mark had run down the stairs into Ernie's office to search for some method of starting the fire, found nothing of use but picked up the bags of money along with the passports and took them out to place in the van. In the glove box he found the spare lighter and aerosol can. He quickly locked the vehicle and ran back inside the building. Before going back up the stairs he went into Ernie's office once again and retrieved two spare magazines for his gun from the desk drawer.

In his haste to start the fire, Mark had not noticed that in his absence a small pool of petrol had seeped into the carpet and gathered around the base of the door. He squatted down on his haunches, holding the lighter and aerosol can, one item in each hand. He became aware of the small pool of petrol at the same instance that he pressed the aerosol spray. But he couldn't stop the other reflex action of his right hand holding the lighter, even though a full flame did not erupt from the lighter the single spark was sufficient to start the conflagration.

However, Mark's quick reactions did save him from being caught in the main body of the backlash. He pushed himself up from the squatting position and managed half a step backwards.

His back was pressed against the balcony rail with such force that the ageing woodwork gave way under his weight and he fell off the balcony with a startled yell.

At the same time as Mark fell, Natalie let out a scream on hearing a whooshing sound as flames shot out from under the door and quickly moved across the concrete floor. The door was also engulfed in flames. Natalie was trapped on the other side of the room. She gathered her senses and tried to operate the fire extinguisher but couldn't get it to work. Vic, seeing her struggle, shouted out, "Stand back Natalie, I'm coming over," and without hesitation he ran forward and leapt over the ever expanding flames, nearly knocking Natalie over when he landed beside her.

He grabbed the extinguisher from her and got it working after a few moments, then started spraying the foam over an area of fire just in front of them. He briefly turned to Natalie. "I'm making a safe barrier through the flames. When I say go, run through as quick as you can. Ready, Go!"

Natalie dashed through the gap in the fire and Vic followed behind carrying both extinguishers. As they reached temporary safety, Natalie let out another stifled scream and pointed towards the area of wall below the louvre window. Ernie was also staring wide-eyed at the same area, first mumbling and then shouting in ever-increasing volume, "No", NO, NOH!"

They briefly saw the outline of an elderly tall man standing in front of the wall, and just as suddenly he disappeared. On the wall there appeared the chalked frame of a doorway with four large circles and inside each of the circles was a large cross. On the floor where the figure had stood moments earlier was the same sticky substance he had seen before, that now slowly disappeared. Vic was the first to react: "Natalie, put one of those dust masks on yourself and Ernie. They're not perfect but they should help a little. Then try to keep the fire under control as best as you can with the extinguishers."

He took a mask for himself, put on the goggles and picked up a sledge hammer.

Mark would surely have been killed by his fall if it hadn't been for the position of the settee; as it was, even though the furniture softened his fall he still bounced off and landed on his right foot at an acute angle. This put too much pressure on his Achilles tendon and it gave a popping sound as it severed. Mark's second yell of pain was not heard by the occupants of the room above.

Vic had made some progress with the sledge hammer and to his relief discovered that there was only a plasterboard skin on the inside of the wall he was attacking. Then he discovered why the apparition had marked four circles on the wall. There was a vertical cross of heavy timber in place to support the plasterboard and he would have wasted precious time and energy if he had attacked the wall at those points.

Natalie started coughing as the smoke built up in the confined space, and realising the problem Vic switched his attention to the window above the door. A couple of blows with the sledge hammer made light work of the glass aperture. The smoke that had built up around the ceiling started to be drawn out by the draft.

Mark had lain on the floor for more than a minute, unable to move because of the acute pain in his ankle. Two things made him stir.

The first was the dull thudding coming from upstairs. He cursed when he remembered the builders' gear and guessed what they were doing in the room.

The second event to make Mark move his position was more pressing. Pieces of burning material were starting to drop down from the balcony above, one landed on the part of his jacket covered in petrol and it started to smoulder. He managed to get the clothing off as small flickers of flame started to rise from the material. Even so, he sustained a few burns to his hands when retrieving the gun and magazines from one pocket, but couldn't find the van keys. He flung the now burning jacket into a corner. More burning embers fell onto the settee from above and Mark hobbled away but was distracted by someone else arriving at the Centre.

Sergeant Proudfoot had seen smoke starting to billow from the broken window as he approached the building and could hear the repeated hammer blows coming from the same vicinity. He hammered on the door with his fist and called out, "Police! Is anyone in there?"

On hearing the shout Mark moved to a position where he could have full view of the front door and when Proudfoot repeated his call he started shooting. But after two bullets were discharged the gun clicked empty. However, he had some limited success with his shooting, one bullet had hit the policeman in his left bicep. Mark turned around with the intention of reloading his weapon but the settee was now engulfed in flames and acrid smoke was billowing around the interior of the building. He hobbled towards the rear exit to avoid being overcome by the fumes.

12

Proudfoot was not badly hurt but he knew better than to try and tackle a gunman by himself. Instead he summoned help over his lapel radio, calling for all blue light services and notifying them there was a gunman in the building.

Vic had also heard the shots and paused for a moment to catch his breath and check on how Natalie was coping.

"How much longer, Vic, I don't think there's much left in this extinguisher."

"I've started to dislodge the bricks on the outer skin of the wall so hopefully a few more minutes should be enough. Use what foam you have left to keep the flames away from those boxes of perfume, if they catch fire we'll have big problems."

"I'll try my best but you may have to pass me that second extinguisher pretty soon."

He looked briefly at Ernie who was now looking grey and only breathing very shallowly. Vic picked up the sledge hammer and renewed his assault on the wall.

***

Mark had managed to find an old three-quarter length hooded raincoat that had been left behind by one of the

Centre's visitors; putting the coat on, he hid the gun in one of the pockets after replacing the empty magazine with a fresh clip. As well as being a form of disguise the coat would cover some of the burns he had sustained on his arms when his own coat caught fire. They had started hurting but nowhere near as much as his ankle, which made him grimace if he put too much weight on it.

He spotted and removed a white walking-stick hanging on another hook by the back door. It was a little short for him but it would have to do; besides, he thought, he would have to stoop slightly as he walked, thus enhancing his disguise.

As he moved out of the building he noticed the banging from upstairs had stopped. With luck perhaps those three sods had finally been overcome by the smoke, he thought, no witnesses left to cause trouble.

He paused briefly to pull up the hood as it had started raining and a strong breeze was now blowing. He was about to close the door but decided not to do so. The wind blowing into the building would fan the flames even more. He moved past the van, cursing his luck at losing the keys and walked across the large car park and turned left onto the main street. By the time he had hobbled fifty yards the sound of approaching emergency vehicles could be heard. At least Gerry's skeleton keys were still in his pocket so he could break into Ernie's flat and lie low until he could plan his next move.

***

Sergeant Proudfoot had decided to move from his position near the door to check if there were still sounds coming from upstairs. He risked taking a quick look through the glass part of the door and was concerned to see black smoke billowing around inside. If the gunman had stayed where he was then he would probably have been overcome by the fumes. Blood was starting to seep through his clothing but he managed to block out the pain for the time being.

Vic had resumed his attempts at demolishing the bricked-up doorway and had nearly made a gap large enough for them to squeeze out. The rubble was in a small pile on the outside balcony. He could now clearly hear the emergency vehicles getting nearer, but would they reach them in time? He gave one more swing of his hammer and a larger piece of masonry joined the rest of the rubble. With a slow creaking groan a ten foot section of the balcony collapsed to the ground twenty feet below.

"Oh shit! What do we do now," Vic cursed.

Natalie had emptied the fire extinguisher and had moved momentarily to kneel by Ernie. She heard the crash of rubble falling and Vic's curses but didn't move from her position. Vic turned to look at her and noticed tears trickling down her cheeks. She looked up at him. "I think he's dead, Vic," she said, and sobbed quietly.

He knelt down to quickly check for signs of life, stood up and gently raised Natalie to her feet and held her in his arms briefly. They both removed the dust masks from their faces. The flames were now only about eight feet away and reached above head height. "We can't do any more for him but we have to make a choice. We can climb through that hole and drop down onto the ground below and hope we don't badly injure or kill ourselves."

"What's the alternative?" she asked shakily.

"You go through the hole and suspend yourself from that crossbeam with the safety harness."

"But what about you, Vic? You can't stay in here."

He took stock of the room to estimate which would be the last place the flames were likely to reach. "I will use the other extinguisher for as long as possible then move into the corner next to you. The fire brigade are pretty close now so it won't be too long before they get to us."

Without waiting for a response he gently manoeuvred her to

the hole at the same time as he picked up the safety harness and slipped it over her head. "Carefully step out backwards through the gap and put your arms around the beam while I secure the harness. That will hold you until we're rescued."

She hesitated only long enough to give him a quick kiss on the lips and followed his instructions. All that remained of the broken balcony was a single plank of wood. Natalie held onto the cross beam of wood, tested the plank to make sure it would hold her weight, ducked under the beam and turned to face Vic as he secured the harness.

Moments later the Chief Fire Officer's car arrived, followed closely by the first fire engine. Proudfoot ran over to the fire officer and told him there were people trapped in the room above. By this time Natalie was suspended from the beam and was in full view of those below. They could also see the smoke billowing out of the window above and around her.

A high wall ran parallel to the Centre and formed a narrow alleyway which prevented a ladder being used as the angle would be too acute. The fire officer instructed two firemen to find a rear entrance to the building. Two more were donning breathing apparatus; another was running out a hose reel.

Moments later one of the men contacted the fire officer by radio saying that there was a door open to the rear but visibility was poor because of the thick smoke. A second fire appliance with a turntable ladder arrived in the car park at the rear of the Centre and was quickly set in position.

Two firemen, one wearing breathing apparatus got into the hoist and were quickly lifted up into position within a couple of feet from where Natalie was suspended. She was coughing and spluttering as the smoke was blowing into her face.

"Not the time or place for hanging around young lady, we'll have you down in a jiffy," one of the firemen called.

His colleague held Natalie firmly around the waist while he unclipped the harness from the beam. She was pulled into the hoist and within a few seconds they were back on the ground. Natalie managed to point back to the area from where she had been rescued and said, between gasps for air, "Vic is still in there near the corner," then she collapsed to the ground. Two paramedics rushed over to assist her.

The hoist was sent back up into position with an extra fireman in breathing apparatus, and additional cutting equipment and hoses.

Vic's plan to use the second extinguisher had proved futile as it had very little foam left inside, so he was now curled up on the floor trying to stay below the smoke but even though he had replaced his dust mask he was having difficulty in breathing. One of the firemen stuck his head through the gap that had been created and shouted to Vic, "Can you move back a couple of feet, mate, we need to make this hole wider in order to get in, and we'll have you out in no time."

Vic had only turned and started to move back when the cutting equipment roared into life and the fire personnel made quick work of demolishing the remainder of the brickwork and wood blocking his escape route. The two firemen wearing breathing apparatus jumped into the room, one operating a hosepipe and the other moved over to Vic. "Hell, there's another one here, Dennis," came the muffled voice from behind the oxygen mask which was removed to reveal an attractive blonde woman. She put the mask over Vic's face and said, "Take a couple of deep breaths, love, and then I'll get you out."

Doing as he was told, Vic managed to gasp, "He's dead, shot."

The firewoman glanced quickly at Ernie, removed the rest of her breathing equipment and passed it to the fireman on the hoist. Before Vic had chance to protest she came back in and picked him up with little effort in a fireman's lift and carried him out to the safety of the platform outside. Placing him in a sitting position on the floor in the corner of the hoist she said something to her other colleague, donned her breathing equipment once more and went back into the building to assist the other fireman tackling the blaze.

The hoist was lowered to ground level and two more paramedics came over to assist Vic who was grateful for their support. The fireman spoke to his superior officer and pointed once more to the upper floor of the building. The Fire Officer nodded, gave further instructions to the fireman who got back into the hoist and raised the platform once more. The Fire Officer beckoned to Inspector Stevens to come over to him, spoke briefly and then walked away, talking into his radio.

Stevens moved over to where Vic was sitting on the back step of an ambulance. He asked if it was in order to speak to Vic for a few moments. After some hesitation one paramedic nodded and stepped back. Stevens turned to Vic, "Holland, I appreciate you've gone through an ordeal but there's a couple of things I need to know. The Fire Officer informed me there is a body in that room up there. Do you know who it is and what happened to him?"

Vic coughed a couple of times before replying in a hoarse voice, "It's Ernie Newsham, Sir, he was shot by his partner in crime, somebody called Mark. He was one of the two blokes who attacked me in that derelict building."

"Newsham? Partner in crime? What the hell are you talking about, Holland?" demanded his superior.

"Ernie was the brains behind all the robberies and break-ins around the area over the past few years. Sorry, Sir, I can't speak anymore, can you tell me where Natalie is?"

"She's in the paramedic's car over there; she wouldn't go in the ambulance that took Sergeant Proudfoot to the hospital."

It was Vic's turn to look puzzled. "Why was Sergeant Proudfoot taken to hospital?"

"He was shot in the arm, not too seriously, probably by the same man who killed Newsham. Do you have any idea what their next move was supposed to be?"

Vic had another coughing fit before replying, "They took some boxes from upstairs after locking Natalie and me in the room. Something was mentioned about loading them into a van."

Stevens thought for a moment. "There's a van still parked out the back. Either the gunman's body is still inside or he couldn't drive the van for whatever reason. If it's the latter he must be on foot and not too far from here. I'll check with the Fire Officer if another body has been found inside. Go over and see your friend, Holland, and then follow the advice of the paramedics." He gave Vic a reassuring tap on the shoulder before walking away.

Having reached the paramedic's estate car Vic asked the driver how Natalie was and could he talk to her. Before the driver could answer Natalie jumped out of the passenger seat and rushed to hold Vic in a tight embrace and started sobbing quietly. Vic returned her embrace and said, "OK, it's over, we got through it, don't ask me how but we did!"

Natalie said nothing, contented with holding on and being held by Vic. The paramedic let them stay in position for a minute and then cleared his throat to attract their attention. "I need to check you out for any injuries and your vital functions, Sir, to see if you need to attend A & E."

Natalie reluctantly let go to allow the paramedic to lead Vic to the ambulance standing nearby. She went and stood in the doorway of the swimming pool to get out of the wind and rain. While he was being checked out Vic asked one of the ambulance crew if they knew the extent of Sergeant Proudfoot's injury.

"Bullet wound in his left bicep just above the elbow, fair bit of bleeding but he'll survive. Stubborn old bugger, he wouldn't go to the hospital until the inspector ordered him to get into the ambulance."

The medic took off the straps and wires he had attached to

Vic's body and arms and told him, "Your vital functions are OK, some smoke inhalation but I would be happier if you went for a precautionary X-ray."

Vic was about to say he felt OK to stay where he was as Inspector Stevens approached. "Holland, can you remember the type of jacket this character, Mark, was wearing?"

Vic thought for a moment before replying, "Bomber style, olive green with red trim around the collar and cuffs."

Stevens went back to the rear door of the building and was handed something by one of the firemen. He returned to Vic and showed him a piece of material. It was part of the lower sleeve of a coat in the colours described by Vic. The upper edge of the sleeve had scorch marks. "This was found in a corner about fifteen feet from the stairs, so it's possible he is injured. The keys to the van were under the burnt-out settee. A gun was also found on the floor with a couple of empty magazines, one nearby and the other by the rear door."

"Both Mark and Ernie had guns, Sir; it's possible that the gun you found was Ernie's."

"Right. Sergeant Proudfoot said he could see smoke inside so if Mark was on foot and injured then he could still be in the general area."

Natalie had been listening intently and she said quietly, "At about the same time the fire started I thought I heard a yell from inside the building. Maybe Mark fell off the balcony and hurt himself."

Stevens turned to her and smiled. "Good thinking, Miss. The fireman said there was a gap in the railing along the balcony. They noticed the gap because the stairs were burnt away and they put their ladder up at that point in order to tackle the blaze in the room from the outside."

Natalie flushed slightly, looked back at the building and commented, "There's less smoke coming out of the building, have they finished putting the fire out?"

Stevens replied, "Yes, they're dampening down. Most of the stock was destroyed."

***

Mark had made slow progress on his damaged leg and he knew there was no way he could get to Ernie's flat without stopping to have a rest. He remembered a place close by where he could hide out until nightfall, which was only about an hour away from Ernie's house. Then there would be fewer nosey people around to be inquisitive about his presence.

He found refuge in a derelict building that was all too familiar to him and Vic, the burnt-out remains of Robin Stockwell's former home. His ankle was giving him so much pain he felt he would pass out if he didn't stop and take off his trainers.

In his journey to his refuge he had been fortunate in the fact that only two people had passed him. One was a blind woman with a guide dog, the other a teenager on a push bike who had narrowly missed hitting him as he rode his bike on the pavement. There had been a brief exchange of insults before the lad rode on swiftly to get home out of the rain. There had also been some traffic passing by but Mark hoped the murky conditions and heavy rain would have occupied their full attention, so as not to notice him shuffling along.

On reaching the derelict building he had hobbled past the boarded-up section of what had previously been a large plate glass window to sit in the corner that would only be visible to someone who ventured in completely through the doorway. It was not the driest spot but it would have to do while he rested his foot. He contented himself by thinking of the money waiting in Ernie's place for him. And the thoughts that the only two witnesses to the killing of Ernie were also probably dead. However, this thought was countered by the sudden realisation that his passport and the other money was locked away in the van outside the leisure centre. How the hell do I get abroad now, he thought, and cursed himself for losing the van keys. He fumbled through the pockets of the waterproof coat he had taken and to his surprise and satisfaction he found a half-eaten bar of chocolate which he finished off in two bites. He took out his gun and placed it close by his side.

He then tried to remove the trainer from his injured leg but just undoing the lace sent red hot stabs of pain up the back of his calf. Letting out a yell of pain and a string of profanities before he could stop himself made him aware of how his voice bounced around the shell of the building. If he wanted to remain hidden he would have to keep quiet.

***

Inspector Stevens, Vic and Natalie were sitting in the foyer of the swimming pool next to the Leisure Centre. Vic asked his superior why Sergeant Proudfoot had come to investigate. "He had a visit from the Potter woman who had been in the area when the travel agent's was destroyed. She gave a good description of someone running away just before the explosion, probably Mark I would guess. Sergeant Proudfoot had a message to say you had left the Golf Club with Ernie and he wanted to know why you hadn't followed his instructions about going back home to write out your statement."

Vic looked a little embarrassed but Stevens continued, "He rang up Ernie at the Centre who denied seeing you at first and then made up a story about being busy and promptly hung up on him. That set some small alarm bells ringing in the sergeant's mind so he came along to investigate."

Vic suddenly remembered the moments before Ernie and Mark came into their room, and hearing what Mark had bragged about doing. "You had better inform the fire service people that they may well find another body in the rubble of the travel agent's, that will be the third member of the gang, his name was Gerry."

Stevens frowned. "Mark's treachery to his former friends knows no bounds it seems. The armed response unit should be arriving soon, in the meantime I'll have to check if there have been any sightings of Mark," and he left the couple by themselves.

Neither spoke for a few moments until Vic murmured, "Nothing has gone right for me since I came to this town, it might be a good time to make a fresh start somewhere else."

Natalie stayed silent, busying herself with stirring her coffee, then she looked at Vic. "Thinking of anywhere in particular? And are you going to stay in the police force?"

"No special place comes to mind at the moment. And as for the police, I still have to prove I'm medically fit. All suggestions considered," he said, looking directly at her.

Natalie looked straight back at him. "Ever thought about Canada?"

"Not seriously considered moving that far but if there was a compelling reason to do so, then yes, I would think very seriously about it."

She moved a hand across the table and put it next to Vic's arm. "How much 'compelling' do you need?" she asked.

Vic put his hand on top of hers, leaned over and kissed her on the cheek "No more, I'm 'compelled' enough now."

They moved their chairs closer together, leaned against each other and began to think what tomorrow might bring. After a few minutes Natalie said, "I don't know about you, but I need to get out of these smoky clothes and have a good long hot shower."

"Me too," Vic agreed, "your place or mine?"

"Well, there we have a problem. I don't have any men's clothes in my hotel and you don't have any female gear at your place, at least I hope you don't!" she said with a giggle.

"What I wear in my spare time is my business!" he replied

with mock seriousness, but couldn't hold his expression and they both burst out laughing. "Come on, my place is within a short distance from here, if you can manage walking about half a mile."

They stood up and walked out of the foyer holding hands. Natalie spoke as they crossed the car park. "I think we need to say thanks to the firemen who rescued us, do you agree?"

Vic nodded. "OK, but keep me away from that blonde fire woman, she may want to carry me off again."

Natalie laughed. "Now don't you worry, I'll protect you!"

They both started laughing but on looking ahead their demeanour suddenly became sombre. A large group of rescue personnel stood in a half circle with their helmets off and heads bowed. Natalie looked enquiringly at Vic. He pointed at the hoist which was being lowered slowly to the ground.

The blonde firewoman and one of her colleagues stood to attention on the platform and lying between them was the unmistakable shape of a body bag. Ernie's remains were picked up and put into the back of a waiting hearse. Once the task was completed the service teams dispersed to finish their duties.

The Chief Fire Officer walked over to Vic and Natalie "How are you two feeling now? You had a lucky escape, fires that involve petrol often claim victims."

"We're OK now, thanks to your team."

As Vic finished speaking, the firewoman joined them and enquired, "Both got your breath back now have you?"

"Yes, especially thanks to you. I've never been picked up and carried like that," Vic said.

Another fireman called over, "Carol's always picking up men and carrying them away. We're still searching for some of the bodies," and a chorus of laughter spread amongst the fire crews.

Carol spun around and quietly pointed a finger at the commentator and nodded her head just once. Another member of the crew piped up, "That's it Douglas, you'll have to be marked down as 'Missing in Action' next," and he received the same reaction from Carol. She turned to Natalie, "Little boys and their fantasies, they never learn do they?" And with a smile she walked away to join her team to help in clearing away their equipment.

Inspector Stevens joined the couple as they walked slowly across the car park. "The armed response team is in the area now but we've not had a confirmed sighting of Mark. However, a passenger on a bus said she saw a man of about the same build in a hooded raincoat about forty minutes ago who was limping very heavily. And this man had a slight confrontation with a lad on his pushbike. This woman was certain of her facts because the boy on the bike is her younger brother. It's the only lead we've got so it's being checked out."

"If you don't need us to hang around, Sir, we would like to go home and have a shower and change out of these smelly clothes," Vic said.

"No, you go ahead, I know where to find you if needed. I can get you a taxi if you need one, I'm afraid we can't spare a patrol car to take you home, we're a bit stretched at the moment," the inspector replied.

Natalie interjected, "Actually I would like to call in on Jenny Potter briefly, just to say thank you. After all, if she hadn't visited the police station and spoken to your sergeant, it's possible that nobody would have noticed the fire until it was too late."

Vic nodded. "Good thinking, Natalie, we can always call a taxi from her house."

Stevens agreed. "As long as you are both OK to walk in this foul weather. Obviously I'll need statements from you both but that will have to wait until we find and detain Mark."

The three shook hands and the couple started walking in the direction of Jenny's house. The rain had eased off to a light drizzle but the wind had increased significantly. Litter and wheelie bins were being blown about on the streets.

***

Mark had also noticed that the strength of the wind had increased. He was now cursing the fact he had taken his trainer off his foot, it would be too painful to try and put it back on. This plan had not worked and there was no plan B he could think of trying.

13

A head popped up from beneath the floorboards about six feet away from where Mark was slumped against the corner wall. It was the scratching sound he heard that had first attracted his attention. Street lighting shone through the window of what had been the room above. The beam of light highlighted a rat, which was the size of a Springer Spaniel dog, about to climb out of the hole in the floor. It moved its head around slowly, taking in its surroundings and checking for signs of danger or some food source.

The sewer stench of the rodent reached Mark and he had to force himself not to vomit but the rat's keen sense of smell had detected Mark and it turned to face him. The rodent and the human stared at each other.

Mark had a fear and loathing of rats ever since his older brother had forced him at the age of ten to go with him on trips to the large refuse dump on the outskirts of Halifax in search of anything of value they could find and resell. At first Kevin, his brother, would take him onto the rubbish dump to help pick up and carry items home. But on their third trip they disturbed a couple of rats scavenging for food and one of the rodents scampered past Mark so closely the young lad fell back screaming. His brother just laughed and left him sobbing on the ground until he gave up his search for any items of interest.

On their next trip to the dump Kevin took along a .22 air rifle and taught Mark to shoot, using the rats as target practice. This was his first introduction to guns and he refused to go with his brother unless he could take the rifle with him. In later years Kevin introduced him to more powerful weapons that he used in armed robberies and other violent acts. The love of guns would eventually lead to Kevin's death in a confrontation with the RCMP in Canada.

***

Vic and Natalie had arrived at Jenny Potter's house with the intention of saying a brief thank you for her indirect involvement in them being rescued. But Jenny had no intention of letting them leave so quickly, she insisted they come in despite their protestations about needing to get out of their dirty clothes. "No, no you must come inside, there is someone I want you to meet. I can put some old towels on the furniture for you to sit on." And she took Natalie's hand and led her into the living-room where a middle-aged lady sat stroking one of Jenny's cats which sat next to her.

It took several seconds for Vic to recognise the woman as he had only seen her previously standing in a dimly lit porch, then he remembered their brief meeting. "Of course, you live in the apartment below me, but I'm sorry, I've forgotten your name."

The lady stood up and shook both their hands in turn. She had a warm, friendly grip. "My name is Gemma Watson and you are correct, Mr Holland, we do live in the same building," and turning to Natalie she took hold of both her hands, "and you, my dear, are Natalie, Robin Stockwell's granddaughter."

Natalie looked surprised at first and then glanced at Jenny

who had just come back into the room carrying two large towels. "Oh, Jenny has been filling you in on my details."

"A little, but she doesn't know all your secrets. I was a pupil of your grandfather's and he taught me most of my talents including mediumship, clairvoyance and the gift of healing. I go on lecture tours and have recently come back from Canada. But I've decided to give the tours up for the time being, and with Jenny's help re-establish dear Robin's healing circle."

Jenny spoke for the first time. "It's so exciting, and perhaps we can invite that ex-policeman, Ernie Newsham, to join us."

Vic and Natalie looked at each other and in that brief exchange Gemma sensed there was bad news in the offing. She turned to their host. "Jenny, my dear, I'm sure these two guests would welcome a cup of tea and biscuits, or even perhaps some of your lovely cake? If you go and put the kettle on I'll come and help you in a moment."

Jenny agreed and headed for her kitchen, closely followed by the older of her cats. Once she was out of earshot Gemma turned to Vic. "Ernie is not going to be able to join us is he?"

Vic nodded and spoke quietly. "No, he was shot and killed this afternoon and we narrowly escaped a similar fate."

Gemma took hold of one of Vic's and one of Natalie's hands in her own. "You two sit down and gather your thoughts, I will take Jenny's mind off the group we are planning and break the news about Ernie to her at a more appropriate moment." And giving both their hands a little squeeze she left to join their host in the kitchen.

When they were on their own Natalie murmured, "I don't want to hang around here longer than necessary, let's have a cup of tea and make our excuses to leave."

Vic nodded in agreement. They sat down together on the settee which Jenny had covered with the towel and as soon as she did so Natalie's lap was occupied by the younger of the house cats purring loudly. Jenny and Gemma returned a few minutes later, both carrying trays of food and drink. Seeing the cat on Natalie's lap Jenny commented, "Someone doesn't want you to leave, Natalie."

Vic cleared his throat. "We appreciate your hospitality, Ms Potter, but we both need to go home to shower and put on some clean clothes."

Gemma was about to respond when they heard a loud bang outside. Both Vic and Natalie recognised the sound but Jenny thought it was something else. "Oh, those children and their fireworks, have they no thought for the elderly and their pets? I've a good mind to phone the police."

Vic stood up and asked his host, "If you show me where your phone is I'll phone them for you."

"Would you be so kind, it might come better from you Victor, the phone is in the hallway."

Vic left the room, closing the living-room door behind him.

***

Mark and the large rat had warily watched each other for several moments until the rodent turned its head to one side to briefly eye something on the floor. Lying less than a foot from his right leg, Mark spotted the carcass of a pigeon. To reach the carcass the rat would have to virtually step over his injured foot. There was no way he was going to let that happen, memories of his youthful experience of rats flooded back.

Almost as if it could read the human's thoughts the rodent bared its fangs and put its two front feet on the floorboards in position to push itself up from the hole.

Mark was in pain, his lower half was soaked through and he shivered with cold. If the rat came out of its hole it would be out of the beam of light and he wouldn't have a clear view of its movement. He picked up his gun, took deliberate aim, shot the rat in the head, and it fell back beneath the floorboards.

The sound of the gun being discharged seemed to reverberate round and round the shell of the building forever. Some dust and small pieces of masonry fell to the floor near the doorway to his left, followed seconds later by a single brick tumbling down.

He knew it would only be a matter of time before his hiding place was discovered. But they wouldn't take him without a fight. No, he owed that much to Kevin. It doesn't make any difference that it was the Canadian police who shot his brother, shooting the local pigs would even up the score in his view.

***

Vic dialled 999 and when asked which emergency service he required he gave his name and police rank and number. When asked for details he replied, "I'm in 42 Somerset Street, almost opposite the old derelict building and I heard a shot coming from that building. Inspector Stevens of Oldgate station informed me that an armed response unit is in the area and I believe the person they are seeking is in that same building. One other thing, the fire service may also be required because of the unstable nature of the structure."

The dispatcher repeated Vic's message and said he would get Inspector Stevens or someone else to call him back on the number he was calling from. Vic was told to stay where he was, on no account was he to approach the area from where the shooting had taken place, and to expect to be visited by someone from the armed response unit.

Having ended the call Vic returned to the living-room and found Gemma deep in conversation with Natalie. As he closed the door Gemma looked up and said, "Natalie was telling me about the apparition you saw when the fire started, is that the first time you have witnessed such a thing Vic?"

Not wishing to be drawn into the theme of the discussion he asked, "The noise just now, you do all realise that it was no firework but a gun being discharged?"

Jenny was the only one to react. "Surely not, Mr Holland, nobody uses guns around here, this is a very respectable neighbourhood!"

Vic had difficulty in suppressing a smile but continued, "I'm sure it is, Miss Potter, but there are people around who have guns who show no respect for such things. Now, I've spoken to the emergency services and they will be arriving very soon. When they do, they may want to talk to me but they will ring your phone first, Miss Potter, to let me know when they want to speak to me. In the meantime, nobody is to go outside and it would be safer if we all stayed away from the windows, downstairs or upstairs."

Jenny asked pensively, "Is there going to be more shooting? If there is I don't want my cats to go outside until it's safe."

"It's really down to the gunman, the police will try to negotiate with him to give himself up without resorting to force. But it could take time and we may have to wait a while."

Jenny stood up and announced, "Well I hope it won't take too long, I like to be in bed before 9.30 and I only have one spare room for guests. Now, would anyone like some chocolate cake? I baked it this morning before going out to the library but I never got there because of the explosion."

All three accepted her offer of further culinary goodies. Gemma started to ask Vic something but was interrupted by the phone. He guessed it would be more questions on the lines of her previous attempt regarding apparitions and was grateful for the distraction. He managed to grasp the phone just as Jenny was about to pick up the instrument. He picked it up and pointed to himself so that Jenny understood.

"Hello? Yes, speaking. OK, I'll come out now." He turned to Jenny who had tried to listen to the conversation and said, "I'm going outside the front door to speak to someone but nobody else must be visible so make sure you all stay in the living-room until I come back in."

He waited until she had gone to tell the others before opening the front door and stepping outside.

"Constable Holland?" asked the officer standing just inside the gate. Vic nodded. The man had a rifle that fired rubber bullets in one hand and a large pistol in a holster on his waist. "I understand you can help us with some details of the layout of the derelict building across the way?" enquired the officer in a broad Scottish accent.

"Apart from the fact there's a large hole in the middle of the floor that I fell through when I was trapped in there by the same bloke you're after. It wouldn't surprise me if more of the floor is rotten from all the exposure to the weather. I'm not aware of any other way out apart from the front doorway, but I wouldn't like to venture in without adequate lighting."

The officer nodded a couple of times, "Aye, laddie, it's as we guessed but there's no way me or my team are going in after him, the fire brigade say the whole building is unsafe and declared it out of bounds. At least until this wind drops." As if to emphasise his point another gust of wind sent another wheelie bin clattering down the street. "Anything you can tell me about this Mark character? Could he be reasoned with?"

Vic didn't hesitate. "So far today he's killed three people, tried to kill me and a friend, shot and wounded my sergeant, blown up a travel agent's shop and nearly burnt down the town's leisure centre. He's about as stable as that building."

"Well, it's his call then. If he doesn't decide to come out and give himself up pretty soon he's found his own burial spot. Right then, everyone stays indoors until we give the all clear. Goodnight, laddie."

The officer was a big man but he was nearly blown off his feet when the next gust of wind blew down the street. Vic was standing partially in the shelter of the doorway and he had to grab hold of the frame to stay upright.

Even if Mark had chance to scream as the gale hit the corner of the building it was not heard over the roar of the falling masonry. The entire corner façade of the brickwork collapsed inwards with only the odd brick landing on the pavement outside the perimeter of the old chemist's shop.

The armed officer turned to Vic. "I guess they don't need us around anymore. Goodnight again," and he walked briskly to join his team further down the street.

Vic stood in stunned silence for several seconds and glanced to his left to observe his three friends looking out of the window at the carnage across the road. Almost as if by some signal the wind dropped to no more than a very gentle breeze. Clouds of dust rose slowly from the wreckage and drifted upwards.

Only four people saw more than clouds of dust rising. Above the range of the street lighting they witnessed the several clouds merging together into one shape for about five seconds before dispersing. The shape was that of an old, thin man turning towards the watching group, an arm raised in a farewell salute before the breeze picked up once again and the form disappeared.

14

Vic returned indoors after staring for a few minutes at the large mound of rubble that had once been his temporary prison. He found himself thinking how ironic it was that Mark had been drawn back to the same place. As he entered the room Natalie rose and walked over to stand by his side. "Jenny, you've been a very kind host to us but Vic and I really do have to go now in order to shower and get out of these dirty clothes."

Gemma stood up and spoke. "I think that's wise, dear, my car is parked around the corner. I'll give you both a lift and then come back to stay with Jenny for the night. She's feeling a little nervous after today's events. I can collect some overnight things when I drop you off at your flat."

They knew to argue or refuse the offer would be pointless so they nodded their thanks and appreciation. Gemma turned to Jenny. "I'll also bring back those books I promised you. I shouldn't be more than an hour as I have a small diversion to make on the way. If you can have a cup of hot chocolate waiting for me when I return, that would be wonderful, my dear."

Jenny nodded and spoke to the couple. "Thank you for coming to see me tonight. If you can wait one moment I'll wrap up a couple of pieces of my cake. There's far too much for Gemma and myself to finish."

Natalie and Vic thanked Jenny for her generosity, retrieved their coats and put them on. However, before allowing the guests to leave, the two cats spent several seconds rubbing themselves against their legs. Jenny clapped her hands together and the cats reluctantly moved away. "Fish and Biscuit, you must let them go home now, I'm sure we will see them again soon."

Vic and Natalie smiled, nodded in agreement and stepped outside. Across the street, the fire crews were erecting a large screen to obscure the view as they went about the grim task of retrieving Mark's remains. Vic briefly caught sight of Carol, the firewoman, picking something up and passing it to a policeman standing nearby.

The couple sat in the back of Gemma's car and as she drove off she looked at Natalie in the interior mirror. "Which hotel are you staying at, Natalie? I'll take you there so you can pick up an overnight bag, or am I being a little presumptuous?"

"No you're not, and that would be fine. It's the Majestic on George Street," Natalie replied, giving Vic's hand a slight squeeze which he returned.

They travelled in virtual silence for ten minutes until Gemma drove into the hotel car park. "We'll wait here for you, Natalie, Vic and I can have a little chat while you collect your things. Don't rush, collect all you need for your stay."

Vic had wanted to go into the hotel but he resigned himself to what he expected was coming. After Natalie had disappeared into the foyer of the hotel Gemma turned around in her seat and looked at him with a friendly but determined look on her face. "What's bothering you, Vic? Why are you avoiding talking to me about recent events?"

Vic was taken a little aback by the directness of her questions. It took him a few moments to reply. "I didn't want to talk about

Natalie's grandfather because it upset her last night in my flat when the subject was brought up."

Gemma nodded. "Naturally it would, but she is a strong woman, don't underestimate her resilience. Actually, I was talking more about your own experiences, what you have witnessed and the details of your own background that have come to light."

Vic sat open-mouthed as Gemma continued, "Please, tell me about everything. I promise I won't laugh, make fun of what you say or try and baffle you with weird explanations."

Vic was tired and he didn't have the energy to argue or deny that he was unsure of what to make of some of the events that had taken place. So he started from the beginning. He spoke of the fire in the now demolished building and how he was rescued, the cream that had been put on his hands by Robin Stockwell's apparition, causing his burn wounds to disappear in a matter of days.

Then he went to talk about the second apparition who claimed to be his sister, Janet, and the letter that arrived confirming what he had been told. "I forgot to mention that I had been put on a course of tablets by my GP. Except that the tablets delivered to me contained some substances that led the doctor into thinking I had been on drugs. I was almost relieved when he mentioned drugs because the symptoms I experienced matched the effects that the substances could have caused. I was having hallucinations caused by these drugs and that was the answer, no ghostly visits! Until the letter arrived and destroyed that theory."

"Didn't you find something in your bathroom cabinet next to your tablets?" Gemma asked quietly.

"Oh, the lighter. Jenny must have told you about it, but I don't remember saying it was in the bathroom cabinet."

"Well yes, she actually said you found it in a cupboard, do you still have it?"

"No, I left it with the police but I hope to get it back so it can be given to Natalie. It's probably the only possession of her grandfather's that's left."

Gemma nodded in agreement and after a short pause she said, "There's still something bothering you about these events, especially knowledge of your sister, even though you have written proof in your mother's letter."

Vic looked around to see if there was any sign of Natalie returning but the rest of the car park was deserted so he spoke in a husky voice. "If she died as a baby then why did she appear to me as a full grown adult? And when she, or should I say, her apparition touched me, why did it feel solid? It was the same as when Robin's ghost picked me up and moved me in the derelict building. How could a ghost pick me up and carry me? And that cream on my burns, why isn't it available to other burns victims? I want to believe and accept those things actually happened, but logical thinking tells me they couldn't have done so."

It was Gemma's turn to look around before speaking. "Even in the psychic circles I work in there are varying opinions as to whether babies and children who have passed over remain in the same state. Some psychic practitioners firmly believe they do, others, and I am one, believe it's an individual choice of the entity to develop or not.

"Let me ask you something Vic. If the spirit world needed to warn you or make you aware of an event that was going to happen in your life, would you believe a total stranger? Or someone like, say, a long lost relative?"

"Well, that ghost was a total stranger to me. If the message was so important why couldn't the ghost of my mother deliver it?"

Gemma gave a faint smile. "Can we use the word spirit instead of ghost please, Vic, I'll explain why. Over the centuries many parents have used the idea of ghosts to keep their offspring in check. Just like older children sometimes do the same to scare their siblings with stories of ghosts and other horrible things that might happen to them.

"You know, we are all born with some psychic abilities but over the years these abilities wane if they are not allowed to develop naturally, or the child is not believed by others if they say they see things that other people don't see. They get ridiculed and sometimes frightened out of telling the truth, so they suppress their talents and over time these talents disappear through lack of use.

"The spirit of your sister visited you because, perhaps for some reason, your mother could not face you. She may have been frightened you would have been angry or upset with the message she had to bring. Some people are frightened by spirits and the same can be said for some spirits, they only want a positive outcome from their visit."

Vic blushed slightly as he remembered his reaction to the letter. Gemma continued, "As for the visitors' solidity, those spirits who were gifted on Earth with psychic talents would still have those powers and would be able to visit us when they felt it necessary."

Vic thought he had found a flaw in Gemma's explanations and put up a hand to speak. "But my sister died at birth, she wouldn't have these talents as you call them."

Gemma smiled and shook her head. "You've forgotten what I told you a few minutes ago. Your sister, like the rest of us, was born with these talents and she grew up, or more correctly, developed in the spirit world where there is no denial of such things, therefore her spiritual development would be stronger.

"Let me finish explaining before Natalie returns in a minute or so. As I said, their spiritual powers allow them to return in their original form. Or in the case of your sister, in the form she would be now if she had lived. The solidity is created by a substance called ectoplasm. Did you notice anything strange once their forms disappeared?"

The memory of the sticky substance suddenly became fresh in Vic's mind and he nodded slowly. Gemma continued, "That is the remains of ectoplasm but as you probably noticed it disappeared very soon after your visitor left you."

There was a tapping on the driver's door window; they both turned to see Natalie standing there with an overnight bag in one hand and a dress cover on her other arm. Vic got out and opened the boot of the car and placed the overnight bag inside and laid the dress cover on top. He gave her a quick peck on the cheek and whispered, "I've just been given the grilling I was hoping to avoid but I do feel better for it."

Natalie smiled, said nothing and returned his kiss, and they both got into the car.

Gemma asked Natalie if all was well in the hotel.

"I did get a few funny looks when I went in to reception in these dirty clothes and then came back down without changing. I think the porter thought I was doing a runner until I explained I had been invited to a party and would not be coming back this evening."

"Can I come to this party with you?" Vic asked with a smile.

"If you play your cards right I might consider you," she replied with a wicked leer.

Gemma laughed and drove out of the hotel car park. By the time she pulled up outside Vic's apartment he was having difficulty in staying awake. All three got out of the car, collected Natalie's belongings and stood in the entrance hall.

"I need to collect a few things before I return to Jenny's, but before I leave you there are a couple of items I need to mention to each of you," Gemma stated as she stood at the foot of the stairs, thus blocking the couple from passing.

"Natalie, forgive me if you already know this but I believe your grandfather owned his shop and flat. It's obviously just a pile of rubble now but I am given to understand that a number of developers have been pestering the council to find the owner of the land. You, being the sole surviving descendant of your grandfather, are now the owner of that land and can sell it to whoever you choose."

After giving Natalie a kiss on both cheeks, Gemma turned to Vic. "As for you, Vic, there is more paperwork to arrive which will benefit you in a small way. And now I will leave you both to recuperate and get to know each other better. When you have decided where your futures lie I would love to meet up sometime."

Vic then received the kiss on both cheeks and a quick hug before Gemma opened her apartment door and went inside. Vic retrieved his keys, picked up Natalie's bag and led the way upstairs to his apartment. Placing Natalie's baggage on the settee Vic asked, "Do you want to have the first shower while I check the freezer for a meal?"

"Wouldn't we save water by showering together?" she asked innocently.

"We would, but it's only a small cubicle and we might get stuck in there together."

Natalie put her arms around his neck and said huskily, "And I suppose we would have to call the fire brigade and your friend Carol would have to rescue you from me."

"And who would rescue me from Carol?"

"Oh, I'm sure that could be arranged, for a consideration," and they laughed, embraced and shared a long, lingering kiss.

Vic gave her a playful tap on the rear. "You go first while I rustle up some food," he said, attempting to withdraw from her embrace but Natalie held on and whispered, "I'm hungry, but not for food, Mister."

"Then you'll have to curb your appetite until we've both had a shower, Miss," and gave Natalie another slap on her rear. She released him and turned and walked to the bathroom with a seductive swing of her hips. All Vic could think of saying was, "Wow!"

By the time Vic had finished his shower, Natalie had dried

her long hair and was waiting in the large double bed for him to return. He was wearing his bathrobe and he looked at her and said with a smile, "You really are hungry aren't you?"

She threw back the bedclothes to reveal her nakedness. "Why don't you come and find out!"

He did. And they both satisfied their relative hunger long into the night, unaware of the two female ghostly visitors who briefly watched over them as they slept in each other's arms in the early hours of the following morning.

Dawn broke that late November morning, crisp and clear, with no trace of the previous day's inclement weather. By the time they rose from their bed the frost had melted away. After a light breakfast Vic took Natalie for a walk in the park and then they stopped in his local pub for a lunchtime drink.

Being a Saturday it was quite busy so they had only planned to stop for the one drink. But news of their dramatic rescue had spread and they were bombarded with questions about the events of the day. Vic managed to avoid going into too much detail with the excuse that it was still part of an on-going investigation, which did have an element of truth. However, this didn't stop a few people buying them more drinks in the hope of loosening their tongues. But they held firm and managed to extract themselves after an hour.

On their return to the flat Vic checked his mailbox and found he had one item of post that had a familiar postmark and handwriting. In the flat he dropped the letter on the coffee table and went into the kitchen to make them a hot drink. Natalie was fast asleep, curled up on the settee when he returned with their beverages so he decided not to disturb her. Instead, he sat in the armchair and picked up his letter.

It had the same format as before, a short letter with an additional envelope inside, so he followed the same procedure, letter first and check the other contents later. This time the letter didn't divulge bad news. The Matron of the home wrote,

"Mr Holland, you may remember in my last letter I informed you that the belongings of your late mother's cousin were sent to local charity shops. I was passed the enclosed envelope by a woman who had purchased a handbag from one of the charity shops. She found the envelope in a zipped compartment of the handbag which was missed when we checked before disposing of it. Thinking it may be important she returned it to me and I forward it to you with my profound apologies that it was not noticed previously.

Yours sincerely,
Miss D Popperwell – Matron."

Looking at the second letter he noticed it had a strange crest on it that he couldn't quite make out. Opening the envelope he found a letter with the same crest which was a lot clearer. It belonged to a well-known legal firm in London. It was addressed to his mother's cousin and read as follows:

"Dear Ms Denman,

We are seeking to make contact with Mrs Irene Holland or her descendants as a matter of urgency. Her late husband, Mr Arthur Holland, made regular payments into an endowment policy for several years. These contributions were matched by his employers until Mr Holland's untimely death.

Having been taken over by another company these details have only just come to their attention and in the intervening years, even though payments ceased at the time of Mr Holland's death, the policy has continued to accrue interest on its capital.

As part of the conditions of the merger of the two

companies every effort must be made to contact all outstanding policyholders, Mr Holland being the last unaccounted person on our list.

If you know the whereabouts of any descendant of the late Mr Arthur Holland, or you are aware of any such person(s), please ask them to contact the above telephone number quoting the reference number before 31 December to justify their claim.

If no person comes forward by this date, under the terms of the merger agreement, the company has the right to claim those funds as their own."

Signed by a Mrs Clare Timson.

Vic sat back in the armchair and tried to think back to the times before and after his father's death. He was only twelve years old when he was told the devastating news. After leaving the army when Vic was still only a toddler, his father worked as a bodyguard-cum-chauffeur for a security firm and travelled the world looking after clients. There would be occasions when his father was away from home for several weeks, sometimes months at a time. But when he was home he told Vic stories about some of the places he had visited and always brought gifts for his mother and him.

Vic sat deep in thought and didn't notice Natalie had awoken from her slumbers until she said softly, "Penny for your thoughts, or has the price gone up lately?"

Vic turned and smiled. "No charge for these thoughts," and passed her the letters. She read the main letter twice before passing them back to him. "I was thinking back to the time when we heard the news about my father's death. It seems he had a heart attack when visiting Canada, Vancouver, I believe, with the MD of an oil company."

"Vic, there's your Canada connection. As I told you last

night, I've got an apartment in Vancouver, it's a big friendly city but with plenty of countryside all around to explore."

Vic smiled. "And the perfect guide to show me. But we have a few things to sort out here first. Apart from this letter and your inheritance and what you intend to do, statements to make about yesterday's events and whether I want to go through a fitness test to stay in the police."

Natalie slipped off the settee, knelt beside him and looked directly into his eyes. "Oh, after last night I can vouch for your fitness! But are you having second thoughts about wanting to leave the police? I could recommend you to the RCMP if you like."

He playfully ruffled her hair and knelt forward to kiss her on the forehead. "No second thoughts about leaving the police, but the Mounties? I've never had an affinity with horses or them with me, and I don't like wide-brimmed hats."

Natalie got up and sat on his lap and whispered in his ear, "This may come as a surprise to you, buster, but the Mounties now use things like automobiles and helicopters and I've always had a thing for men in wide-brimmed hats!"

"Well in that case, wench, I think it's time for another fitness test" and he pinched her on the rear.

Natalie let out a little yelp, stood up and looking over her shoulder poked out her tongue at him. "Catch me if you can!" She ran towards the bedroom, followed closely by her suitor.

15

They spent the rest of the weekend enjoying each other's company and making plans for their future.

Venturing out to a local restaurant for Sunday lunch proved not to be a good idea; as in the pub the previous day they were conscious of other diners watching their every move. Things came to a head when the third pair of drinks were brought to their table by the waiter with a message. "Compliments of the lady and gentleman on table seven, with many thanks for getting rid of those thugs."

Vic turned and gave a wave in the direction of their benefactors, turned to Natalie and whispered, "If it's OK with you, I would rather give the dessert a miss. This is getting a little embarrassing."

She nodded in agreement and after finishing their main course Vic went to pay the bill. The manager of the establishment refused to accept any payment and said the meal was free with his compliments. Vic asked why they were being treated as minor celebrities by everyone. The manager replied, "Those people who died as a result of your actions were nothing less than a mini mafia around here. People were too frightened to go to the police and they knew it."

Vic went back to his table and slipped a couple of ten pound notes under a plate to cover part of the cost of their meal. Natalie stayed silent until they were outside. "Hey, big spender, do you always tip so generously?"

Vic replied, "They wouldn't let me pay the bill but I can't be seen accepting freebies, no matter how good their intentions might be. If people were too scared to tell the police then I see that as the force failing in its duty."

"Another reason to leave here and move on?" she asked, on their way back to the flat.

Vic simply nodded, deep in thought.

The ringing of the telephone woke Vic the next morning. There was no sign of Natalie and he hadn't been aware of her leaving the bedroom. He picked up the receiver and the voice of Inspector Stevens came down the line. "Ah, Holland. Can you and Miss Jardine come down to the station this afternoon to make your statements? I would like to have this investigation completed as quickly as possible."

Vic was about to answer when Natalie popped her head around the corner of the bedroom door; all she appeared to be wearing was an apron. "How do you like your eggs, sunny side up?"

Vic gave her the thumbs up and spoke into the receiver, "Can we make that late morning, Sir?" I have a couple of important phone calls to make first."

"Make it twelve noon, oh, tell Miss Jardine a couple of people have been trying to contact her rather urgently. See you at midday." And the line went dead.

Vic got out of bed, retrieved his dressing-gown from behind the door and went to find Natalie in the kitchen. He stood in the entrance for a moment to admire the view. He had been correct in his initial assumption, only the apron covered her modesty. "That apron looks much better on you than me," and he went over to where she was standing by the cooker and gave her a light kiss on one shoulder.

"You can have it back to do the washing up after. Now sit down while I serve up our breakfast."

Moments later she placed a plate filled with a full English breakfast adorning it. He stared at the meal and said, "Where did all this come from? I haven't had any sausages, bacon or hash browns in the freezer for weeks while I've been trying to lose weight."

She smiled as she put her own plate down on the table. "I called in the supermarket we passed on the way back from the restaurant, and you need to keep your energy level up, so get eating!"

"What, dressed like that?"

Natalie said nothing, she just smiled and gave him a little wink. They sat and ate in silence and when Vic had finished, he sat back in his chair and said, "Wow! I didn't realise how much I missed the naughty food, and so well cooked, thanks."

Natalie finished her own meal, wiped her lips with a serviette and spoke in a husky voice, "Well, if you'd like to show your appreciation I'll be waiting in the bedroom!"

Vic shook his head. "Sorry, I'll make it up to you tonight; we have a busy morning ahead of us: phone calls to make and a visit to the police station to make our statements."

Natalie took off the apron and stood in front of him, "Are you sure you don't want to change your mind?"

Vic moved away from the table. "Tempted as I am, not this time. Besides, someone has been making enquiries about your whereabouts at the police station. I'm keen to find out who is my rival for your attention."

Natalie looked puzzled. "Someone asking for me? Nobody else knows me in this town apart from Jenny and Gemma."

And then the realisation dawned on her. "Gemma said something about my grandfather's old shop and possible redevelopment of the area. Do you think it's about that?"

"Only one way to find out, but before doing so I need to phone this solicitor in London."

It took three attempts before he was finally connected to Clare Timson, the solicitor dealing with his father's estate. Despite giving the reference number on the letter and other details, it was only after telling her that he was a serving policeman that she agreed to talk in more detail. But she wouldn't disclose the value of the inheritance until she had seen the relevant certificates of birth and marriage and other documents. Fortunately Vic had retained all these items.

He was given a choice of sending them by post or personally delivering them to the solicitor's office in London. He put his hand over the receiver and called to Natalie, "Fancy a trip to London in the next couple of days?" She nodded her head vigorously and Vic arranged a time and date for their trip. After discussing a few more details with the solicitor he put the receiver down.

"Going to London was part of my travel plans for when I came here, with a trip to Scotland if I could fit it in," Natalie said, as she finished getting dressed.

Vic joined her in the bedroom and commented, "It might only be a day trip to London, and Scotland is a bit nippy at this time of year, it is November after all."

Natalie gave a hearty laugh. "Nippy? If you mean cold, Mister, we have plenty of real cold in Canada. When I get you over there, first stop is the ski slopes."

Vic smiled to himself; he and Fiona had gone on a couple of skiing holidays in Switzerland during their marriage and he had impressed the ski instructor with his ability. *Someone is in for a surprise when we get to Canada.*

Vic collected his car from the garage and was relieved it started at the first attempt. He drove them to the police station as the weather had changed yet again with sudden squally showers giving a more autumnal feel. It was also an opportunity for him to give his car a much-needed run to charge the battery. They agreed not to mention anything about the vision of Natalie's grandfather appearing in the room just after the fire started. Vic knew none of his colleagues had any time for unexplained ghostly appearances.

Arriving at the front desk at the police station, Vic was greeted by one of his colleagues with the comment, "Oh yeah, we've heard all about you and that firewoman, looking for protective custody are you Vic?"

Before he could reply, Natalie gave the constable a withering smile and said, "Sounds like your friend is a bit jealous, Vic, perhaps no woman has wanted to carry him away."

The young officer coloured slightly and passed Vic a pen. "Sign in and I'll call the inspector."

The couple went to sit on a bench to wait to be called. "How did you guess?" Vic asked.

"Guess what?" she replied.

"Roger is gay," he answered and it was Natalie's turn to blush.

Before the conversation could develop any further Inspector Stevens arrived and invited them to follow him. He enquired if they had both recovered from their ordeal and both answered in the affirmative. They were led to a pair of doors which had 'Interview' and a number on them. "Miss Jardine, if you go into room two a WPC will be along shortly. Holland, you can use room three and I'll send someone in to you. It's a busy time, Sergeant Proudfoot is in room one and he would like to see you before you leave the station. I will need to have a word with you both as well."

Vic gave Natalie's hand a little squeeze before they parted and went into their respective rooms.

He finished giving his statement before Natalie and was ushered into the inspector's office. "Well, Holland, you seem to have come out of your ordeal relatively lightly, no adverse health issues to add to your previous adventures?"

Vic shook his head and was about to speak but Stevens held up a hand for silence and continued, "Good, because your fitness assessment has been set for two weeks from today. Unfortunately, with Newsham's death there is nobody to run the Leisure Centre and swimming pool so you won't be able to take advantage of those facilities to prepare yourself for the check-up."

Before the inspector could say any more Vic spoke, "Excuse me, Sir, I have decided not to put myself before the medical board. In fact I intend to resign from the force as soon as it can be arranged."

Stevens sat in stunned silence for a few moments before speaking. "Resign? Why? I am sure you would get through the medical without too much trouble, but if by any chance you didn't pass sufficiently fit for frontline duties, I'm sure we could find you a desk job. In fact, how would you fancy promotion to sergeant and take over the front desk?"

It was Vic's turn to find himself temporarily lost for words so the inspector continued talking. "Sergeant Proudfoot is also resigning, he feels he wants to move on to something different. I believe he's interested in taking over Ernie's Newsham's role at the Leisure Centre. Which reminds me, did Newsham give any indication to you why he turned to crime?"

"He was bitter about not being able to re-join the force after proving his fitness following the car crash, while Proudfoot was promoted to sergeant and kept on, despite being partly responsible for the death of two other people.". But there's something else you ought to know about Ernie's crime wave."

Stevens sighed but let Vic continue. "Over the weekend Natalie and I have been to a number of places around the town and from what was said, people were too scared to tell the police what was happening to them. They simply didn't trust us, I got the impression people felt if they approached the police it would get back to Ernie and there would be repercussions."

Stevens held up a hand to interject. "Don't say any more, Holland. We found details in both the safe and at Newsham's place to confirm he was blackmailing a member of the police authority into informing him of any police activity in relation to all the break-ins and arson attacks that have happened here and in other parts of the force area. That person is being interviewed under caution as we speak."

Before Vic could respond a knock was heard on the door and Stevens called for the person to enter. "Miss Jardine has finished giving a statement, Sir, and you said you wanted to speak to her," said the WPC and showed Natalie into the room, closing the door on leaving.

Natalie sat next to Vic and gave him a little smile.

"I hope that wasn't too taxing for you. You will both understand that your statements will have to be compared so there are no discrepancies and that either one or both of you may be asked to come back to iron out any points that need clarifying."

The coupled nodded as the inspector continued. "Now, Miss Jardine, there are a couple of things I need to tell you. Firstly, the local council planning department are anxious to talk to you about the plot of land that was once your grandfather's shop and flat. Here is the name of the person you need to contact," and he handed Natalie a sheet of paper. He then reached into a drawer in his desk and took something out. "Secondly, as no charges can be brought against anyone who is still alive concerning your grandfather's death, as his only surviving relative I need to pass this item onto you."

He handed an envelope to Natalie who opened it a little pensively, and when she saw its contents let out a little gasp. "Oh, thank you, thank you," was all she could say, while holding tightly onto her grandfather's gold cigarette lighter. A couple of tears ran down her cheeks and Vic passed her his handkerchief and held one of her hands.

The inspector stayed silent for a few moments before speaking. "Holland, I almost forgot, I have something here you may be able to identify for me. Do you recognise this?" and he passed a large clear plastic bag containing one trainer shoe with a silver buckle on the outer edge.

Vic nodded. "Yes Sir, that's one of the trainers worn by Mark."

"When the walls collapsed there wasn't much left of the body for identification purposes but the rubble seemed to have pushed that to the surface. It was the first thing the fire crew found at the site."

Vic held the bag for a moment and then handed it back to his superior and said, "I call that poetic justice."

Stevens nodded and stood up to shake both their hands. "That's it for now, there are a couple of minor details to be sorted, not least a submission to the coroner's office to have the verdict changed on your grandfather's post mortem. And, Holland, you will need to contact the personnel department if you are serious about your early retirement and iron out pension details. Now if there's nothing else, I have another meeting to attend. Oh, don't forget the sergeant is hoping to see you before you leave."

Proudfoot was waiting for them by the reception desk he normally occupied and as soon as he saw the couple, approached them and turned his back to the desk so that nobody else could hear him speak. "Glad to see you are both OK, I'd like to have a talk with you Victor about recent events. But I would prefer to make it a more private venue, too many ears around here."

Vic was taken aback by Proudfoot's mellow tones, but more by the sergeant's use of his first name; he could not recall it ever happening before in the whole time he had spent at the station. He lowered his voice and replied, "Where do you suggest? One of the local cafés, or we could go back to my flat."

Proudfoot hesitated before replying, "Well, if you don't mind, I was thinking of my place. My wife dropped me off here on her way to work at the hospital so we won't be disturbed."

Vic looked at Natalie who nodded her agreement. "That's

fine but is it OK for Natalie to come as well, otherwise I'll take her back to my flat and you can give me directions from there."

"Of course Natalie is welcome along. Oh, by the way my name is Peter Proudfoot," and he extended his good hand to Natalie who shook it gently. His right arm was in a sling to protect it after the shooting.

All three went back to the desk to sign out before departing to Vic's car. Natalie climbed into the back seat to allow the sergeant to sit next to Vic to give directions. There were a few moments of embarrassment as he struggled with his seat belt which ended with Vic having to clip the harness into the buckle. "Thanks Victor, you don't realise how unfriendly the world is to a one-armed person until you end up like this.".

Natalie sensed the frustration in his voice and said softly, "Well, make the most of it, once you get fit again I'm sure your wife will find you plenty of tasks to do."

Proudfoot merely grunted but Vic sensed he would have responded more caustically if he had uttered the same remark. Following instructions he arrived at the sergeant's residence within fifteen minutes and pulled into the driveway of the semi-detached home.

Proudfoot fumbled in a pocket to find his keys and with a few mumbled curses under his breath he finally got the door open. As he stepped into the hallway a large Alsatian dog approached him, wagging its tail furiously. He ruffled the animal's ears and pointed silently and the dog turned and went to sit at the bottom of the stairs. Showing his guests into the lounge he indicated to Vic to sit on the settee and turned to Natalie. "I wonder if you could do the honours by making a pot of tea? I'll show you where everything is kept, as well as Mrs Proudfoot's hiding place for the biscuits."

Natalie smiled, nodded and followed him to the kitchen. Moments later the Alsatian came into the room and sat on its haunches a few feet in front of Vic; it just sat and stared at him with unblinking eyes.

Proudfoot returned, and after observing the two occupants for a few seconds he went to the dog, pointed at Vic and then himself, then gave the thumbs up sign. The dog relaxed and went to sit next to the armchair in the bay window, which Proudfoot then occupied. Vic was first to break the silence. "Doesn't the dog understand voice commands, Sarge?"

"We're both out of uniform, lad, so please call me Peter. No, Gellert is deaf due to an incident when she worked in the police dog team in a neighbouring force. Nobody else was prepared to give her a home so I stepped in. We've had her for about three years now."

He ruffled the dog's ears once again and Gellert was about to put her head on the arm of the chair when Natalie walked in with a tray laden with teapot, cups and a packet of biscuits. It was the latter that caught the dog's attention. Noticing the reaction Peter pointed in turn at the biscuits, his guests, himself and finally at her. Gellert put her head on the arm of the chair, this time with a mournful look on its face. All three humans let out a laugh.

Vic had moved a coffee table into the centre of the room and Natalie placed the tray on its centre. She sat next to Vic, allowing the tea to brew for a few minutes longer. Peter picked up the plate of biscuits and offered them to his guests before taking one himself. Gellert looked at him with pleading eyes and when Peter held up one finger the dog sat up and held a paw up for his master to shake. After releasing the paw he picked up a single biscuit and placed it gently on the end of the dog's nose who stood impassively waiting for the signal.

Peter took a couple of bites from his own biscuit before nodding his head. Needing no second bidding Gellert flicked her biscuit up into the air and deftly caught the treat between its teeth and then went to lie down at her master's side. The party trick earned much laughter from Vic and Natalie who then got up and poured the tea. She passed a cup to Peter and Vic before sitting back down with her own drink.

After a couple of minute's silence, Peter became suddenly serious and asked, "Victor, did Ernie Newsham give any clue as to why he went off the rails? I've known him for years and he was a stickler for playing by the rules. Granted, he had his problems from time to time but never to the extent of breaking the law to such an extent."

Vic cleared his throat before speaking; he didn't know how his host would react to what he was about to tell him. "Sergeant, sorry, Peter, just before Mark came into his office, Ernie was holding a gun on Natalie and me and he was feeling pretty resentful about you and how the force had treated him after the accident. He claimed that even though you were driving the car that night you had some element of blame for him being crippled out of the force and you gaining a promotion."

Proudfoot held up his good hand. "Stop right there! I wasn't driving the patrol car, Ernie was, and what's more his blood was found to contain more than the permitted level of alcohol . He had taken to drinking vodka between shifts after his marriage ended. Yes, the other car jumped a red light but if Ernie had been stone cold sober he could have avoided that accident, his reactions were too slow. When he regained consciousness after the accident he couldn't even remember he was doing the driving.

"He was lucky he wasn't prosecuted for drunk driving and causing death by reason of being unfit to drive. There was no way the Force would take him back after that. I tried to help him as much as possible but he kept asking me why we were going so fast when the accident happened. He didn't remember we were on an emergency call at the time.

"I got him that job at the Leisure Centre through my contacts on the Council and you weren't the first person I sent to him to regain their fitness."

Vic sat in silence for a minute before speaking again. "OK, you were there and I can only tell you what Ernie said, but something else is bothering me. When we were in the Botany Bay restaurant yesterday the owner told me people were too afraid or didn't trust the police to tell them about the break-ins and things that were going on. Why or how could this happen?"

Proudfoot finished his tea and put the cup back onto the tray before responding. "On the rare occasion that anyone made a complaint about those two thugs, Ernie would step in with the perfect alibi for them. Of course, at that time we had no idea that he was co-ordinating the whole racket, but over the past weekend evidence has been found both at the Leisure Centre and at Ernie's place listing all the activities they were involved in. As well as bank accounts in foreign countries set up to pay out monthly payments to each of them. At the last count there was over a quarter of a million pounds in those accounts and that didn't include the bags of cash found in their van."

Vic let out a low whistle and Natalie sat in stunned silence. "Has anyone searched Andrew Phillips's house yet? He told me before he died that he kept details of the air ticket and Canadian currency bought by Natalie's grandfather, that was stolen when his house was burgled and set on fire."

Vic could see that his last remark had come as a surprise to Proudfoot so he continued, "Jenny Potter always claimed that the fire was no accident but she had no proof. The evidence that Phillips had, and the cigarette lighter I found, is the proof that foul play was involved. Ernie told Mark that Robin Stockwell had collected Canadian currency and an airline ticket that afternoon; it would too tempting for Mark to ignore."

Proudfoot nodded but then asked, "This Mark character would have known that Ernie and Mr Stockwell were friends and that Ernie would have stopped him if he knew what was about to happen?"

"That's what everyone thought but another thing Jenny told me was that Robin Stockwell had voiced his misgivings about Mark and Gerry, and Ernie had lost his temper when confronted by Robin. You're also forgetting, Ernie drove down to Heathrow that same evening to fly to Australia, leaving the way clear for Mark who had other plans for that money and ticket.

"Another thing they mentioned was the death of Graham Bishop. Mark admitted his brother, Kevin, drowned Bishop in the swimming-pool before dumping his body in the river. It's all in my statement and another verdict the coroner will have to change."

Proudfoot let out a long sigh. "At one time Bishop was one of our prime suspects but we found no evidence to implicate him."

They all sat in silence for what seemed like an age before Proudfoot finally spoke. "It seems I, along with a few others, owe Jenny an apology for not taking her seriously regarding this matter."

"I'm sure she will be very pleased to hear you say that. Jenny may be a little eccentric but her heart is in the right place," Natalie added quietly.

Proudfoot smiled as he said, "Oh, I'm sure she will love me eating some humble pie. Well, I'll make that one of my last duties before I leave the force in a couple of months."

"Leaving?" Vic asked

"Surely you must have a few years left before you are due to retire," Natalie said.

Proudfoot nodded. "Oh yes, my dear, at least six years before the official date but I've decided to go now while there's an alternative post in the offing. Once the Leisure Centre is repaired and a few alterations are made I've been unofficially offered the chance to take over from Ernie. It's an opportunity that's too good to turn down. I've got an interview later this week. And you won't have me making your life a misery, once you've passed that medical in a couple of weeks."

It was now Vic's turn to reveal his future plans. "Well, I'm afraid you wouldn't have had chance to keep me on my toes anyway, Sarge. I'm leaving the force as well, I'm moving to Canada with Natalie once we have sorted out a few loose ends here."

"Are you sure, Victor? Moving abroad is a big step to take, especially if you've never been to that country before."

Vic held Natalie's hand and gave it a little squeeze. "I see it more as grabbing the opportunity before it disappears, and I'll know at least one person who will act as my guide."

"Well, I can see there's no point in me trying to put you off the idea but let me give you one piece of advice. Make sure you get your police pension sorted out before you go abroad, it's tricky enough when you're not in the same town, let alone another country."

This last comment signalled to Vic that it was time to end their meeting, there were other things to be sorted and time was pressing so he stood up followed by Natalie. "Thanks for the tea and biscuits, Mr Proudfoot, but as well as Vic's pension I have a couple of matters to sort out myself before we leave. I'll take the tray back to the kitchen and wash up if you want."

"Please call me Peter, and no, I can manage the tray and we have a dishwasher that even I'm not allowed to touch. My wife will be back soon." And as he finished speaking a car pulled up in the driveway next to Vic's vehicle. "That's Marjorie now, she's a bit earlier than normal. Oh well, she's caught me with the biscuits again, Gellert."

The dog must have sensed the arrival of the car and sat up next to Proudfoot who stood up and led the way to the front door. All three waited in the porch for Mrs Proudfoot's arrival, when introductions were made. Marjorie was a short, slim woman but had the air of someone who would not tolerate any nonsense from anyone.

"You're back early dear?" enquired Peter.

"Yes, one of the X-ray machines has developed a fault so there was no point me hanging around." She looked past her husband at Gellert who had followed the trio.

"Feeding the dog biscuits again I notice, he'll be putting on weight just like you Peter." Everyone else looked slightly puzzled at the remark. "He's got crumbs on his muzzle and I thought policemen were trained to notice evidence!" she said with exaggerated patience.

Vic and Natalie took the opportunity to leave the sergeant to defend his actions and held back their laughter until their car was out of sight of the Proudfoots' house.

16

Natalie spent a couple of hours later that afternoon speaking to officials in the planning department of the borough council to find out which developers had shown an interest in her grandfather's old shop.

There was a reluctance on the part of the Chief Planning Officer to even discuss the matter until she produced proof of her relationship to Robin Stockwell. Once that had been established his manner changed and he arranged a meeting with Ralph Byewater of Byewater Construction PLC for the following morning.

After enjoying another of Natalie's cooked breakfasts Vic accompanied her to the meeting in order to give her moral support. On their arrival they were greeted by a short bespectacled man in his late fifties. "Miss Jardine, I'm so pleased to meet you. I was beginning to despair whether the rightful owner of the land in question could ever be found. My legal people were having discussions with the council about having a compulsory purchase order put on the old shop but I was a little reluctant to take such a course of action."

"Why so, Mr Byewater?" asked Natalie.

Byewater hesitated, looking a little embarrassed, before

speaking. "Please call me Ralph, Miss Jardine. I knew both your grandparents for many years and they were like family to me at times. One of my sons also benefitted from their, shall we say, unique gift and talents."

"And you may call me Natalie. In what way did your son benefit?"

"He was asthmatic from an early age and all the medical staff could offer him was an inhaler to help ease the condition. Your grandfather made up a special linctus for him to take daily. After three months he was completely clear of asthma. There were many other instances I can recall where my family was helped by those two kind people.

"Let me be frank. I, like so many others in this town owe a great deal to your grandparents and I would not have wanted to obtain the land belonging to them without paying its full market value to their descendants, namely you, Natalie."

"Can I ask how much would that be?" Vic asked.

"I don't have the latest valuations of property in that area to hand but the last time I checked it was in the region of £85,000."

Natalie let out a gasp. "Really? Why so much?"

"One of the main providers of sheltered housing for the over-fifties is keen to move into the area, they have already bought other derelict buildings nearby. The old chemist's shop is the prime site that's holding up the development and they are prepared to pay any asking price for the land."

"How long will it take for the necessary paperwork to be drawn up to complete the sale?" Natalie enquired.

"I can have the papers ready for you to sign in the next couple of days and, say another fortnight to complete the transaction. Does that fit in with your plans?"

Natalie turned to Vic. "That would give us time to fit in a visit to Scotland after your trip to London on Thursday. Are you game?"

Before Vic could respond Ralph interjected, "Whereabouts in Scotland were you thinking of visiting?"

"Anywhere near or in the Highlands, I've heard Perth is a nice place to visit."

Ralph gave a little laugh and said, "I happen to own a chalet that's part of a time-share complex owned and run by an international company called Diamond Resorts. They have several sites in this country and many more mainly in Europe and the United States. This particular one is on the banks of Loch Tay in a village called Kenmore by Aberfeldy. It's less than one hour's drive from Perth. I would be very honoured if you would be my guests and stay up there for a week. You will have the chalet all to yourselves and I can give you details of places to visit in the area."

The couple were stunned into silence for a few moments, but after exchanging glances they both nodded and Natalie said, "Thank you so much, that's very kind of you, we would love to go."

"Good, that's settled, I'll arrange for the keys to be ready to be picked up from the reception desk in the complex. Oh, and you will have free access to all their facilities under my full membership rights. You said you were visiting London on Thursday; if you call back here on Friday I'll have the papers ready for you to sign and give you directions to Kenmore."

They all stood up, shook hands and the couple left the office unable to believe their good fortune. In the car, on the way back to the flat Natalie said, "Everyone around here is so kind, are you sure you want to leave?"

Vic nodded. "The kindness you're receiving is all based on the goodwill built up by your grandparents. They must have been quite a special couple."

Natalie smiled in agreement.

The next day, Vic set the ball rolling for him to resign from the police and put the wheels in motion for sorting out his pension as Proudfoot had suggested. Inspector Stevens had tried once more to persuade Vic to stay on with a hint that he could take the sergeant's place provided he sat and passed the necessary exams to qualify. But there was no chance of him changing his mind, he knew his future lay with Natalie in Canada.

On the Thursday morning they travelled to London by train for Vic's appointment with the solicitor. The meeting was completed rather quicker than Vic had anticipated, once he had provided the necessary proof of his relationship to the satisfaction of the solicitor. A number of papers had to be signed and counter-signed and he was told a cheque would be sent to him within the following ten working days.

His father's pension was not a vast fortune but, along with his savings from the sale of his parents' old house, it would be something to fall back on if he didn't find early employment when they moved to Canada. The rest of the day in London was briefly spent in going around some of the sights and shops Natalie had wanted to visit.

It was nearly midnight when they arrived back in the flat, exhausted but happy after their hectic day in the capital. As a result they overslept the next morning but were eventually woken by the persistent ringing of the telephone. Ralph Byewater's tone sounded a little concerned when he spoke to Natalie. "Oh, I'm sorry to bother you Natalie but can you come over in the next hour to sign the papers and collect the instructions to get to the chalet. A small family crisis has arisen and I have to leave the office by midday and I won't be back until after the weekend."

"OK, we'll be there in half an hour, is that alright?" Ralph confirmed that was acceptable and Natalie had to give Vic a little poke in the ribs to waken him from his slumbers.

They completed their business with the developer and returned to the flat to prepare for their trip to Scotland. Natalie called at her hotel to collect some more appropriate clothing she had brought with her from Canada. While she was busy doing her packing in the bedroom Vic checked the best route to take and noticed the name of a place they would be travelling through. On the spur of the moment he made telephone enquiries about using that as a possible stopping point on the way. The journey to Kenmore would take the best part of ten hours so it was decided they would leave early the next morning.

Heavier than usual traffic and bad weather made a stop necessary at the village Vic had selected, just over the border in Scotland, as both of them were feeling tired. An evening meal and bed and breakfast was arranged at the hotel Vic had chosen. As Natalie had her eyes closed when they drove into the village, she wasn't aware of its name or significance.

The next morning after breakfast she suggested a short walk around the village before they continued their journey but Vic persuaded her that it would be more beneficial if they got back on the road fairly quickly, just in case they encountered more traffic or weather problems. He did relent by suggesting they could always stop there briefly on the way home, which satisfied Natalie.

Fortunately this part of the journey was completed within four hours which allowed them time to stop in Perth to do some necessary food shopping before taking the winding uphill road to Kenmore.

On the approach to the time-share complex they passed a large old building named the Kenmore Hotel which was next to an iron road bridge crossing the river Tay and marked the start of their final destination. Vic presented the receptionist with a letter of introduction from Ralph Byewater and was handed the keys to the chalet along with a message from the developer. "Mr Byewater hopes you have a happy and restful stay in the area; there is a bottle of wine in the fridge, with his compliments, and could you inform him when you decide to travel back home."

The receptionist explained about the facilities they could

use on site and gave them a booklet describing some of the places to visit in the area. Finally she gave directions to their chalet. This was situated near the banks of the loch and from the balcony on the upper floor, which housed the living area, they had a magnificent view across the loch to the mountains beyond. The spacious accommodation consisted of three bedrooms, all ensuite, and a sauna room on the ground floor, while upstairs was a large kitchen and dining-room with a table to seat eight people.

Dusk was approaching when they had finished their unpacking and as they stood on the balcony to admire the view they were surprised by an unusual sound which Natalie recognised first. It was the sound of the bagpipes being played by a lone piper standing on the shore of the loch. The couple held hands and smiled wistfully at each other and remained, listening and watching until the piper had finished.

Their food shopping only consisted of breakfast and light snacks, so they were fortunate to have booked a table for the evening at the site restaurant.

Natalie had finished changing into her evening clothes and was about to close the curtains and lock the balcony door when something outside in the distance caught her attention. She let out a small squeal of delight and called to Vic to come up from the bedroom immediately. Sensing something was amiss he bounded up the stairs in just his shirt and underwear, which amused Natalie.

"Not quite the dashing white knight I expected but you'll do. Look!" and she pointed outside.

Vic stared, unsure what he was supposed to be looking at, and said, "At what, that firework display? What's so special about a few fireworks?"

"Fireworks! That's no ordinary fireworks Mister, that's nature's fireworks! Haven't you heard of the Aurora Borealis, the Northern Lights?"

It was Vic's turn to call out, "Wow! Yes I've heard, but never seen it until now."

"Well, get used to it Vic, we see it on a regular basis every year I've been in Canada, although this is a bit late for it to appear."

They watched in amazement until Vic checked his watch and pointed out the time to Natalie. "Sorry, but it's time to move, we're already late for our table booking."

Natalie looked him up and down. "Something of yours is going to get mighty cold if you go out like that and you won't be much fun later on."

Vic looked down at himself; he had forgotten about finishing getting dressed, so he dashed back downstairs to complete the task.

It was only a short walk to the restaurant but a cold wind had picked up and they were glad to reach the warmth of the building. The restaurant was busy but they were shown to a table which afforded a little privacy in the corner next to a window. The next couple of hours was spent eating a fulfilling meal, washed down by a couple of bottles of house wine. They were almost the last people to leave the dining area and the bracing wind had increased which encouraged them to hasten their steps back to the chalet.

Over the following week they explored the surrounding countryside either on foot or by car. Their first visit was to the village of Killin which boasted a stunning waterfall which cascaded around a large outcrop that split the falls into two separate parts. The river was not in full flood but they had to shout to hear each other speak. In the nearby tourist shop they were assured that when the river was in full flood, usually following the spring thaw, it was almost impossible to speak at all because of the incessant roar of the flood water.

An indication that the winter weather would soon arrive was the two large snowploughs parked up ready to try and keep the main roads clear, but despite this the local inhabitants were confident that snow would not arrive for several more days.

A warmer indoor visit encompassed one of the oldest whisky distilleries in Scotland which was situated in the neighbouring village of Aberfeldy. Natalie insisted on buying a large amount of souvenirs to take home to Canada.

On Ralph Byewater's suggestion they paid a visit to the Kenmore Hotel that was within walking distance of their chalet and booked a table for that evening. The hotel had several claims to fame: it had been one of the first hotels to open in Scotland in 1572 and Rabbie Burns was said to have stayed there on his travels. The interior décor was unmistakeably Scottish, with tartan carpets and curtains being the predominant feature. A large open log fire added to the cosy atmosphere which persuaded the couple to make several return visits during their time in the area.

On their final day at the resort they made use of the aquatic facilities to wind down before their journey south. Relaxing in the hot tub they had views of the mountains in the distance which had their first covering of snow on the upper slopes. It was time to head back home.

Vic kept his promise to Natalie about calling at the same village they had stopped in on their outward journey. She smiled to herself as they passed the sign that welcomed them to their destination.

"There's been something I've been meaning to ask you, Natalie," Vic said as they pulled into the car park of the same hotel they had stayed in on their way to Kenmore.

She looked out of her side window to stare at the large sign on the hotel front bay before replying, "Oh? What's that?" in a rather disinterested voice.

Sensing a lack of interest on her part it was now Vic's turn to feel unsure but when Natalie looked back at him there was a broad smile across her face and she burst out laughing at his nervous expression. "Yes, I will!"

"Will what, I haven't asked you anything yet," he stuttered.

"Marry you Mister, that's why you brought me here to Gretna Green, isn't it?"

Vic started laughing and they flung their arms around each other.

"You don't seem surprised, how did you know?" he asked, after they had both stopped to catch their breath.

"You left too many clues back at the flat. You circled the name of this place on the map and wrote tomorrow's date next to it."

"OK Miss Marple, I still haven't had your answer."

"You betcha!" she replied, putting her arms around his neck and drawing him closer to plant a long, lingering kiss full on his lips.

As they carried their luggage from the car to the reception desk Natalie had a sudden thought. "Vic, what are we going to do about witnesses, we don't know anybody around here."

"I believe they can provide witnesses in the registry office for a small fee, a kind of professional witness service I suppose. I'll check that out later," he replied with a smile.

After booking in at the desk they retired to their room and while Natalie showered Vic made a few enquiries and was satisfied with the responses he received. He had one more surprise for Natalie and hoped she would not have too much objection to it, but wondered how she would react. "I'm sure you are aware of the rules of marriage that the bride and groom are supposed to spend the night before their wedding in separate rooms, otherwise it could prove to be unlucky. So I will be moving into a single room at the end of the corridor before midnight."

Natalie stared at him, saying nothing, until she finally realised he was deadly serious. She simply said, "If you think you can last the night without me in your cold, lonely bed that's fine by me. Just for the record, I've heard some of these Scottish hotels are haunted, is that true?"

Her last comment had a hint of mischief in it which did not show on her face. Vic decided to play her at her own game. "It's possible, they'll probably be checking that both parties stick to the rules, or else!"

They focused on each other's face, willing the other to break first. It was a dead heat; it started with slight coughs, a little giggle followed by uncontrollable laughter, ending with them falling into each other's arms on the bed. Natalie was the first to speak. "I don't suppose it would break the rules if we had, shall we say a final cuddle, etcetera, before going our separate ways for the night?"

Vic managed to extract himself from her embrace and stood up. "'fraid it would for two reasons. One, you'll need all your energy for tomorrow night and two, we have a table booked for twenty minutes' time."

Natalie pouted and then said defiantly, "Men and their stomachs! And you'll be the one needing energy tomorrow night, don't think you've been tested fully yet, just wait and see, buster!" and she threw the wet towel that had covered her body since coming out of the shower at Vic as he went to collect the overnight items he would need for his temporary stay elsewhere. He turned just in time to see her turn around and give that now familiar provocative wiggle of her hips but this time he couldn't afford to be taken in by the offer or his resistance might have been broken.

Before leaving his new room he phoned the reception desk with a couple of enquiries and left one message that needed to be passed on to another guest at the hotel.

Vic had selected a table seat that gave him a full view of the entrance door to the restaurant, with Natalie sitting directly opposite him. He glanced past her several times while they were making their selection from the menu and coughed loudly when a couple started to enter the room. On hearing his cough they turned around and walked out again. Natalie looked at him suspiciously. "Are you OK? You've been looking around ever since I sat down. Is there someone else you would rather be sitting with?"

Vic laughed nervously. "Course not, Natalie! I was told the person who is conducting the service tomorrow may pop in to see us to have a brief chat. And there is nobody else in the whole world I would rather be with than you," he said with a disarming smile.

"If you say so; hurry up and make your choice so we can eat and go back upstairs to have our own little chat, etcetera."

After finishing their meal they went back upstairs and as Natalie opened the bedroom door he gently took her free hand and gave it a squeeze. "Sorry, Natalie, I meant what I said, I'm tired after the driving and we both need an early night. In separate rooms!"

She pouted and then a wicked smile shone in her eyes. "OK, Friar Tuck, but I hope you have your truncheon ready in case you have any ghostly visitor."

Vic leaned forward, kissed the tip of her nose and gave her a friendly slap on her rear as she entered her room before replying in the same tone, "I'm saving my truncheon for tomorrow night, Maid Marion, so you better get a good night's sleep as well," and quickly walked to his own room before she could respond.

Both of them managed to sleep soundly that night and each one found a surprise waiting in their rooms on rising the next morning.

17

On the bedside cabinet in Natalie's room a single red rose had been placed along with a simple hand-written message. "For the eternal love you have found."

Before getting into bed the previous night Vic had taken out a small plain package from his bag and placed it on the dressing-table in his room. The contents of the package were very precious to him for it contained his late mother's Wedding and Eternity rings which were the only possessions he had kept in her memory. It was his intention to use the rings in the wedding ceremony later that morning, hoping of course they would fit Natalie's finger. If they didn't he was sure there was room for some adjustments.

Vic awoke the next morning, unaware of what had taken place during the night, showered, shaved and dressed before going down to meet Natalie for breakfast. But she was not at their usual table. When the waitress approached he ordered a light breakfast and a pot of coffee for two.

The waitress hesitated before speaking. "Excuse me, Sir, would the other coffee be for the young lady you were with last night?"

"That's correct, we arranged to meet for breakfast before going for a short walk prior to the ceremony."

"Oh, I see, but the lady has had breakfast and left the hotel about ten minutes before you arrived, saying she was going for a short walk to look around the town."

Vic thought for a moment before replying, "in that case just make it coffee for one please."

The waitress left and returned some five minutes later with his order.

Natalie had decided to take a short walk around the town with the intention of finding a particular item she hoped would be available for purchase. She found the item she was seeking in a novelty shop. After paying and leaving the shop she continued down the street until she came across a ladies' boutique. On impulse, she went in and spotted another item that would complete her wedding attire, paid for her purchase and stepped back outside with a smile of triumph on her face.

About fifty yards away on the opposite side of the street, two figures walking away from her caught her attention. There was something vaguely familiar about them. A large lorry passed by, heading in the direction of the couple. As it slowed down briefly to negotiate a set of traffic lights it obscured Natalie's view for a few seconds and by the time the lorry pulled away from the traffic lights the couple had disappeared, possibly into one of the many shops in that area.

Natalie wanted to try and seek the couple out but after looking at her watch she noticed time had passed by more quickly than she had realised and she needed to get back to the hotel to change into her wedding attire. She turned around and retraced her steps to the hotel.

Meanwhile Vic had finished breakfast and gone back to his room to prepare for the wedding ceremony. He had managed to call in the room occupied by Natalie to collect the clothes he would be wearing. He noticed the single red rose on the dressing-table with the note nearby and wondered who had placed it there. He knew Natalie hadn't brought it with her and she wouldn't have had time to purchase the rose locally.

While trying to work out who else had knowledge of their plans Vic took another look at the note accompanying the rose. He felt a cold shiver run down his spine as he recognised the handwriting. It was unmistakably his mother's writing! He stood staring at the note for about a minute until the sound of a key being placed in the lock of the door snapped him out of his lethargy.

Natalie walked into the room with a look of satisfied triumph on her face; in her right hand was the purchase she had made earlier. On seeing Vic standing by the dressing-table, the gift was deftly transferred into the handbag on her shoulder as she turned away from Vic to close the door.

"I thought we were not supposed to meet up before the ceremony, or are you here for some other rehearsal?" Natalie asked with a knowing twinkle in her eyes. Then she noticed the slightly ashen look on Vic's face. "Vic? Is something wrong, you look as if you've seen…" Her voice trailed off as she realised the truth.

"Ghost? Not so much an actual ghost but more like their calling card." And he held up the red rose and the accompanying note. "That's my mother's handwriting, I'd recognise it anywhere."

"But why should she leave a message for me and not you? I must admit I saw the rose when I got up and thought you had crept in during the night and placed it there."

Vic shook his head and smiled. "No, if I had come to your room in the night it wouldn't have been to bring a rose and leave again."

Natalie laughed, walked over to Vic and put her arms around his neck. "Well, we just might have time for a quick practice to refresh your memory about what you missed."

Vic pulled back while removing Natalie's hands from the back of his neck. "You'll just have to wait, I only came in to collect my clothes for the ceremony; sorry but all other physical contact is out until after, then it's every man and woman for themselves."

She reluctantly stood back and stated, "Man, you will pay for this, your screams will be heard all over the Highlands tonight."

"We'll see who screams the most," Vic replied, and managed to avoid Natalie's attempt to pull him forward. He collected his suit and shirt from the wardrobe and as he opened the door to leave he said, "See you downstairs in the bar in thirty minutes?"

Natalie nodded without saying anything and Vic closed the door and left to return to his room. He placed his clothes on the bed and went back into the bathroom to brush his teeth after breakfast, when a sudden thought struck him. He continued to clean his teeth as he walked back to the dressing-table to check that the envelope he had left there the previous night was still safe.

Instinct told him what he would find, and sure enough the same message he had discovered in Natalie's room had also been written on the envelope at some time during the night. As he picked up the envelope Vic felt a sudden rush of emotion and his eyes began to moisten. After a few moments he carefully placed the envelope next to his clothes on the bed and returned to the bathroom to finish his ablutions, and dried his eyes.

Dressing quickly, he was relieved to find his suit still fitted as he had not worn it for at least two years, the last time was at Fiona's funeral. As he checked himself in the wardrobe mirror the phone next to his bed rang; he walked over and picked up the receiver. "Yes? Vic Holland here."

A familiar voice greeted him. "Hello Vic, just a quick message to say I've left the paperwork at the venue which is next to the Hazelbene pub on the high street in Gretna and we'll see you there as arranged."

"Any problems?" Vic asked.

"None," was the response and the line went dead.

Vic replaced the receiver and smiled to himself. That was the final obstacle to his plans that could have spoiled the whole day. Picking up the envelope containing the rings he inclined his head, stared skywards and whispered quietly, "Thanks, Mum."

The bar of the hotel was empty of any customers, so the barman busied himself by polishing the optics, making sure all labels faced forward. He saw Vic approach and turned to greet him. "Good morning Sir, what tipple can I interest you in on this fine day?"

Vic looked at the range of whiskies on offer and was about to indicate to one label in particular, but Natalie had slipped in quietly next to him and spoke first. "Could we have two Taliskers please?" Natalie said as she stopped by Vic's side and he turned to take a first look at her wedding outfit. She wore a three-quarter-length pale yellow dress with a burgundy sash around her waist. A short white leather jacket with the red rose pinned to the lapel and a pair of burgundy shoes completed her attire.

The barman poured their drinks and said approvingly, "You're a very lucky man if I may say so, Sir, the lady has very good taste. Talisker ten-year-old Malt Whisky is distilled on the shores of the Isle of Skye. If I may suggest, it's best served with a dash of water to sooth the palate?" He held up a small jug of water and Natalie nodded her approval.

Vic smiled, passed her one of the whiskies and raised his own glass in salutation. "A stunning sight to behold and a woman who knows a quality drink, what more could a man ask for on his wedding day?"

She leaned forward and gave him a quick peck on one cheek and whispered quietly, "You scrub up pretty well yourself, Mister, and men in black suits do something really groovy for me."

They touched glasses before taking a sip of their drinks and moved to sit down on a comfy settee in a corner.

"So how do you know about the merits of whisky or shouldn't I ask a lady such a question?"

Natalie smiled. "My stepfather only drinks alcohol at Christmas or on very special occasions and it's always Talisker whisky. He let me try some on my eighteenth birthday and I remember the taste."

Vic took another sip of his drink and noticed that her expression had changed to one of what appeared to be a flicker of sadness in her eyes. "Something bothering you at this late stage?" he asked.

Natalie looked at her hands on her lap before replying. "Just a little thought about no other family members being here to witness our special day," she answered wistfully.

Vic took hold of one of her hands in his own before replying in a quiet voice, "Well, the way things have fallen into place so quickly, I'm sure if there had been any disapproval they would have let us know in their own way."

He glanced at his watch and stood up. "It's time we made a move, it will take us about ten minutes to walk to the venue, that's if you are ready and haven't changed your mind?"

Natalie stood up and finished the rest of her drink in one swallow. "Not me, Mister, lead the way!" and took his offered arm as he finished his own drink in the same manner.

They walked hand in hand down the street to the wedding ceremony venue, blissfully unaware of the two women and a man following at a discreet distance. One of the women was carrying a large box or cage.

Vic and Natalie arrived at the front entrance of the Hazelbene Hotel and were surprised at the rather rundown appearance that faced them. Natalie turned to Vic with a puzzled look on her face. "Are you sure this is the place? It doesn't look as if it's open."

Vic gave her a reassuring smile. "Yes it's open, the new owners are in the process of completely renovating the place from top to bottom. Besides, I couldn't get us booked in for the ceremony anywhere else at such short notice. Trust me, everything will work out fine."

He took her arm and gently guided Natalie through the main entrance. They were greeted in the lobby area by a man dressed in full Scottish attire, kilt, sporran and all. The man gave a slight bow and asked, "You will be Mr Holland and Miss Jardine, I take it?" and after the couple nodded in affirmation he continued, "I have to apologise at the outset that the owner of this establishment will not be in attendance as he and his wife have been called at short notice to appear at a planning enquiry. My name is Alan Ferguson and I will be conducting your wedding ceremony today."

Vic replied, "That's unfortunate the owners can't be here, I wanted to thank them personally for allowing us to have our wedding here at short notice, especially with all this work being carried out."

Mr Ferguson nodded. "I will pass on your message to the owners. Now a couple of matters to be clarified if you don't mind. Do you have the special dispensation form from the Registrar General? And your guests to witness the ceremony, how soon before they arrive?"

Natalie turned to Vic with a look of concern on her face and was about to speak when a voice called out from behind, "We're here, ready and waiting."

At the sound of the man's voice Natalie whirled round to face him as he stood next to Gemma Watson. Just behind, Jenny Potter was standing with her two cats on short leads. Each cat had a little bow tie around their necks. Natalie stared for what seemed like an age before calling out, "Dad? Is that really you?" before letting go of Vic's hand and running to fling her arms around the neck of the tall bearded man.

Frank Jardine let out a deep hearty laugh. "In the flesh, honey. Gemma here let me know what you had planned, so here I am, ready to give you away."

Natalie looked at Gemma standing next to her father and then back at Vic who tried to look totally innocent but failed miserably when he burst out laughing. "You said a little earlier you wanted some family present so now you have, satisfied?"

Getting more confused by the minute Natalie turned to her father. "But I spoke to you a few days ago on your mobile when we were staying in Kenmore and you were still in Canada then weren't you?"

Frank let out another belly laugh. "Only just, I was on my way to the airport when you rang."

Natalie turned back to Vic. "So! You send out invitations before proposing to the bride. I think I'm going to have to keep a close watch on you, Mister, and I've got the very thing to help me."

She opened her handbag, removed a pair of handcuffs she had purchased earlier that morning and deftly snapped one end closed on Vic's left wrist, placed the other end on her own right-hand wrist and closed it shut.

"Now I will know what you're up to every minute of the day," she said with a triumphant laugh.

"I hope you've still got the key for those things, Natalie, or it could prove to be a little difficult, not to say embarrassing at certain times," Vic replied.

"Natalie smiled. "Of course I have the key, but I'll only use it when I think it necessary. Play your cards right, Vic, and it could be sooner rather than later."

Oh, and what might that involve?" he replied, giving the handcuff on his wrist a sudden twist. This movement opened the handcuff and Vic took it off his wrist and smiled at Natalie. "I've lost count of the number of times we had parents come into the police station with their kids who had used these things and then lost the keys. If you had told me what your plans were I could have brought the real thing with me. Now, if everyone is ready I think we should proceed with the ceremony. Agreed?"

He gave Natalie a quick peck on one cheek and led her

over to a blacksmith's anvil, over which their vows would be exchanged. Vic produced the rings from his pocket and much to his and Natalie's relief they fitted perfectly.

After the ceremony was completed the group gathered together in an adjoining room for a few photographs to be taken indoors as the weather outside had changed and a persistent drizzle was now falling. While they waited for the photographer to appear, Vic, Natalie and her stepfather stood aside from Gemma and Jenny to have a quick chat.

"How long are you staying for, Mr Jardine?" Vic asked.

"I'll be staying as Gemma's guest for about a week, then a few days in London before flying back home. You see, Natalie, I have attended some of Gemma's talks on her last few trips to Canada and we kept in contact with each other ever since."

As he finished speaking Gemma came over to stand by Natalie. "I'm sure Frank won't mind me telling you this but I gave him a reading and I made the connection between the two of you, via your mother, and my home town. At that time I didn't realise we would meet up so soon."

Vic and Natalie looked at each other, both having the same thought, was this fate or just sheer coincidence? Before either could speak Natalie felt a light tap on her shoulder and she turned to face Jenny Potter. "I hope you won't mind if Fish and Biscuit appear in one of the photographs? I promise they will be on their best behaviour."

Natalie laughed and bent down to stroke the two cats sitting at Jenny's feet. Both purred loudly, and being the senior, Fish demanded more attention than Biscuit. Standing upright once more, Natalie agreed to Jenny's request. "Of course they can, it will be fun to have them in all the photos."

"Oh no!" Jenny said firmly, "they might get nervous if they are exposed to too many of the flashes from the photographer's camera. After the first photo I will put them back in their cage in the next room, it won't be for too long."

Natalie nodded her acceptance and moved to join Vic who had taken a liking to his stepfather-in-law and was asking him about job prospects in Canada.

"If you're prepared to work hard and can adapt quickly to the lifestyle you shouldn't have any problems. If you are interested in a similar line of work to what you've been doing I have a few useful contacts you could meet," Frank replied.

Vic was about to ask another question but was interrupted by the arrival of the photographer alongside Alan Ferguson who called the group to gather together in front of what appeared to be a large cinema screen. The host asked the newlyweds what scene would they like projected onto the screen as a background picture. "I'm afraid we only have a limited number of scenes to choose from due to the refurbishment taking place, so if you would like to make your choice from these photos I have here I will project your scene onto the screen while Jamie sets up his equipment."

Vic and Natalie looked through the five photos Ferguson showed them. To their surprise one of the pictures was that of Loch Tay situated in the village of Kenmore where they had spent the last few days. Without hesitation they both pointed at that picture as their choice.

Ferguson left the room to set up the projector while Jamie organised the newlyweds and guests into position in front of the screen. Within a few minutes the picture of Kenmore and Loch Tay with snow-capped mountains in the distance appeared on the large screen, and everyone turned to appreciate the stunning view.

Natalie whispered in her husband's ear, "That would be a great place to spend our honeymoon, Vic."

He turned to her and said regretfully, "It would, but I don't want to waste my energy driving all the way back there when we can find somewhere more local."

"But the scenery and location, it's so perfect!" Natalie said, with a slight hint of protest coupled with not a small amount of pleading.

But Vic stood firm. "Maybe another time, but I don't intend spending much time looking at scenery when I have you to admire."

She gave him a wicked leer in response and was about to comment when the photographer asked everyone to stand in front of the screen and the group moved into position to have the first photo taken. Almost as if by some silent command from Jenny Potter the two cats moved to stand in front of Vic and Natalie and inclined their heads to look up at the couple. Immediately after the camera clicked they ran back to their mistress and were ushered out of the room.

Gemma and Frank stood to one side as the couple had a few photos taken by themselves. As the last of these photos was about to be taken both Vic and Natalie felt a sudden chill and instinctively moved closer together, then just as quickly, the temperature returned to its previous level.

When the photography session was completed Alan Ferguson reappeared and asked if everything was to their satisfaction.

"Excellent thank you," Vic replied. "How soon will the photographs be available, my father-in-law would like to order some prints before he returns to Canada?"

If you're staying in the area for the next twenty-four hours I can have the proofs delivered to you by midday tomorrow and you can make your choices before you leave."

"That will be perfect, Mr Ferguson," and he gave the address where they were staying before returning home.

The party left the hotel and walked to a nearby restaurant for a form of wedding breakfast that Gemma had arranged. They stayed at the venue for several hours, enjoying a fine meal and several bottles of wine. Jenny had brought along a small wedding cake she had baked before travelling to Scotland. It was made from a chocolate sponge laced with whisky, covered in butter icing and decorated with two interlocked hearts with the couple's initials underneath.

Natalie was a little intrigued as to how all these preparations had been made before she had even known about the wedding herself, and what would have happened if she had declined Vic's offer of marriage? Gemma smiled and leaned slightly forward in her chair so that only the present company would hear her comment. "Shall we say, I had it on good authority you would accept Vic's offer." Both Vic and Natalie had a puzzled look on their faces before realising what Gemma was implying, and then everyone burst out laughing.

It was late afternoon before Vic and Natalie made their exit to their hotel while promising to meet up at around mid-morning the next day to view the wedding photos. Naturally the newlyweds were the last to arrive, to find a very worried-looking photographer alongside Alan Ferguson. Gemma, Frank and Jenny, on the other hand, appeared quite calm.

"Mr and Mrs Holland, I don't understand what has happened and can only offer my profound apologies," Jamie stammered, "I could have sworn the background picture was clear of anyone else."

Alan Ferguson added, "I've re-checked the scene you chose and it was definitely clear of other people. I was standing just behind Jamie when he was taking the photos and I couldn't see anything wrong at the time."

Vic and Natalie looked at each other, unsure what had gone wrong with the wedding pictures. Natalie asked quietly, "What's wrong with the photos you took? Show them to us please."

Jamie carefully opened the portfolio of photographs and showed them, one by one, to the couple. The first few photos with all present, including the two cats, seemed perfect to the newlyweds.

"What's the problem?" asked Vic.

Without answering Jamie removed the last two photos from the binder and both Vic and Natalie let out a simultaneous gasp. What should have been the photos of the married couple by themselves now showed an additional six people standing behind them. Vic and Natalie said nothing for nearly two minutes, all they could do was stare at the images that appeared on the photos. Vic was the first to speak and pointed at three of the images behind Natalie. "My mum, dad and sister."

Natalie said quietly as she identified the other three, "My mum with gramps and grandma."

They turned to face each other and embraced tightly, tears flowing gently down their cheeks. After what seemed an age, Vic took out a hanky and offered it to Natalie who duly dabbed her face dry before passing it back to her husband who did the same.

Jamie cleared his throat before speaking. "I've tried air brushing the pictures on three separate copies but it makes no difference. I don't know what to suggest apart from retaking the pictures."

"That won't be necessary, thank you. They couldn't be more perfect," Natalie said and gave the bemused photographer a hug and kiss on both cheeks.

The three remaining guests joined them as Alan Ferguson said, "But I was standing right behind Jamie and could see nothing different to the previous shots of just the two of you. Where did those figures appear from like that?"

Gemma stepped forward and asked to see the other photos. She checked each photo carefully for nearly five minutes before announcing, "Mr Ferguson, please take a close look at the background and pay attention to the loch and the mountains in particular."

The manager was joined by Natalie's stepfather and he was the first to speak. "Well, the only thing that stands out to me is there appears to be a lot more snow on the lower slopes of the mountains compared to the full group photos we were in. And in the last picture before our unexpected guests arrived, the snow was back to its original level but a mist haze seems to be floating on the loch."

Ferguson shook his head and commented, "But I took those background photos myself in early Spring and there was very little snow as there had been an early thaw. There was certainly no mist on the loch, as you can see from the original picture," he said, as he produced his evidence. Everyone gathered round to compare the images and after all had viewed them carefully Natalie spoke first. "As the pictures taken by Jamie are our wedding photos, I believe the final decision should be ours, don't you agree Vic?"

Vic nodded in agreement. "However this situation has come about, we couldn't be happier with the outcome so we will accept them with great pleasure. So if you allow us to take all proofs and final copies, Jamie, I will settle our bill in full right away."

Gathering all the prints together as quickly as he could in case the couple changed their minds the photographer presented them to Vic along with the bill he had kept in his inside pocket until that moment. Vic produced his cheque book, filled in the details and handed the payment to Jamie. Both he and Ferguson then bade their farewells and left the couple and their guests to continue talking amongst themselves.

Frank Jardine asked Vic, "If it's not imposing on your time, what are your plans for the next few days?"

Vic replied, "We're leaving later this afternoon and stopping for the night near where I was first based before moving to Clapfield. Natalie is curious to see where I lived before moving. Then it's back to my flat to start packing for our move to Canada. Which reminds me, I haven't given my landlord notice that I'm moving out, that's one more task to add to the list."

At this last remark both Gemma and Jenny started smiling

and Vic looked at them curiously, wondering what had amused them. Gemma spoke first. "Your landlord already knows, Vic, and a new tenant will be moving in once you have left."

It was now Jenny's turn to speak. "You see, Victor, once they start work on the site of dear Robin's old shop and the surrounding area, it will become very noisy and dusty around there and Fish and Biscuit would be very unhappy, so I've had permission to move into your flat once you have moved out."

Vic still looked puzzled and Gemma laughed quietly but said nothing. Then Vic understood. "You are my landlord, or should I say, landlady!"

She nodded and sat slightly closer to him. "Can you remember what the letting agency said to you after you viewed the apartment?"

Vic thought for a moment. "I was told that several people had shown interest in the place but it would be the owner's final decision as to who would be the new tenant. I thought it might come down to a pricing war but I was already at my limit regarding rent. I was a bit surprised when I was offered the apartment with a slight drop in rent."

Again Gemma nodded. "Once I was given the list and details of all the interested parties I laid them out on my table and checked through them thoroughly. There were thirteen in all. I used my talents as a medium to sift through them, as I knew I was being guided to choose someone who would not rest once they had started on a mission."

Vic interrupted her. "Mission? Are you trying to tell me that I was chosen to solve the mystery of Natalie's grandfather's death and that's the only reason I got the apartment?"

Gemma nodded once again. "All the other applicants for the apartment were either couples or not of strong enough character for what was required. Yes, Vic, you were in effect chosen to put right a grave injustice and certain events were pre-ordained to happen. Including, I might add, issues from your past that you needed to come to terms with within yourself. Have you heard the word 'Karma' before, Vic?"

Vic gave a brief nod and Gemma continued. "You needed to resolve those things from the past that will govern your future and in doing so, solve the mystery of Robin Stockwell's death. In turn, you and Natalie were destined to meet."

Smiling at Natalie, Vic replied, "But what if I hadn't taken that route home from work that evening and I hadn't chased those two from the shop? It was all pure chance that I was there at that moment. I could have worked overtime, those yobs could have broken into another shop not on my route home, or…"

Gemma laughed and held up a hand. "Vic, Vic, it happened the way it was meant to, accept it. Look at what you have gained."

Natalie spoke softly, "Would you rather we hadn't met, Vic?"

A look of horror spread over his face and he grasped Natalie's hands in his own. "Of course I'm glad we met, you are my future and I hope I'm yours."

Gemma stood up and said, "And that's all you need to think about, let the past rest and build your future together."

"Fish and chips!" Vic said, and laughed out loud. Everyone looked at him and he continued, "If I hadn't decided to go for a fish supper that evening I wouldn't have been in that street, one of my colleagues had told me about a good fish and chip shop there."

"Well, it looks like the powers that be also wanted to stop you from putting on even more weight," Gemma said, causing everyone to join in the laughter.

"Never mind, Vic," Frank spoke, "I've heard there's a top British chip shop in Vancouver that Natalie can take you to visit."

"And it will only be as a very special treat if you play your cards right," added Natalie.

Once the laughter had subsided Vic said quietly, "I think it's time Natalie and I went back to the hotel to finish packing as we need to head back home in order to put some finishing touches to our future plans."

Farewells were spoken, with promises to meet before the couple's final departure to Canada.

Vic woke up in the early hours of the morning to find himself alone in bed. Natalie was sitting by the dressing-table, totally naked, with a small sidelight shining down on something in front of her. He called out softly, "Something wrong, Mrs H?"

She turned and smiled at him, turned off the light and rejoined him in bed. "Just checking the photos once more, all is well."

"You didn't think they would disappear again after going to all that trouble did you? Come here wench, we've got some unfinished business before the night is through."